A Reckless Life

Tyler Series
Book 2

Michelle Files

INTRODUCTION

Teenage Abbey was brought up in a nice, modest family. But, the temptation of drugs and partying was just too much and she got caught up in it all. After running away and getting a job on a championship horse farm, she meets the handsome, and married, Adam Tyler, and is about to jump headfirst into a whole new reality of secrets and lies. Can she let go of the past and embrace an unknown future?

This novel is book 2 in the Tyler Series and is the prequel to Girl Lost. It is intended to be read second.

Novels by Michelle Files:

Tyler Series:
Girl Lost - Book 1
A Reckless Life - Book 2

For information on any of Michelle's books:
MichelleFiles.com

Copyright © 2017 by Michelle Files

All rights reserved. No part of this publication may be reproduced, distributed, or transmitted in any form, without prior written permission of the author.

Published in the United States by Michelle Files
Edited by Cecily Brookes and BookLovers.pub
Cover Design by Estella Vukovic

This is a work of fiction. Any similarities to actual people, places or events is purely coincidental.

CHAPTER 1

ABBEY

The storm was raging wildly outside and I had never been so scared in my life. When I first got into the driver's seat of the car, there were ugly, dark clouds and I could see that a storm was brewing. However, I could not have been prepared for what actually hit us. It came out of nowhere. One moment, it was just dark and gloomy, then all of a sudden, the winds blew at what seemed like a hurricane force. It was blowing so hard, I was having a difficult time keeping the car on the road. We were hit with severe winds that seemed to come from every direction. Through the darkness I saw a window shutter on the second floor of an old house violently tear away from its hinges and fly through the sky, disappearing quickly. I thought about how happy I was that it didn't hit the windshield of the car I was driving. I felt that it took every bit of concentration I had to keep from being blown away, and honestly didn't know if the car was going to keep four wheels on the road or not. I suddenly had visions of Dorothy, along with her house and dog being lifted higher and higher into the sky.

Then the thunder and lightning came, jolting me back to reality. The thunder was so loud, I nearly jumped out of my seat and gave out a small cry of alarm. My passengers looked at me, but said nothing. They were as terrified as I was. It was certainly nothing I had ever experienced before. It felt like the sky was very angry and was making sure everyone on earth knew it. The roar was deafening. The flashes of light were so brilliant, and so close, that I had to squint my eyes for a moment, not watching the road for a precious few seconds.

Then I realized that the lightning was nothing, because once the rain hit, I could barely see where I was going. The windshield wipers on the car were moving as fast as they could, yet it wasn't enough. Not even close. The rain seemed to come out of the sky in huge sheets of water, like ocean waves, descending down on us so hard and fast that the wipers just couldn't keep up. I had to slow the car way down, I had no choice. We would never arrive at our destination in one piece if I couldn't see where I was going. Only an idiot would be out driving in this storm. I had called an ambulance, but crazy enough, there were none available. I was told that it could be two or three hours before one was available. Seems the heavens were tormenting everyone that night.

Because I could barely see in front of me, I was driving slowly when I came upon some debris in the road. If I had been driving faster, I would have surely hit it, stranding us there. I didn't even want to think about that. Unfortunately, there was no way to go around the debris, so I had no choice but to get out and move it. My passengers were in no shape to help me really, and didn't offer. I didn't even look their way. It was all on me, that was clear. As I opened the car door I cursed to myself for being so stupid to not take the time to grab a jacket when I left the house. I was only wearing a pair of jeans, tennis shoes and a t-shirt. As I got out, I was instantly drenched. Then a big gust of wind hit me and slammed the car door so hard, I would have lost a hand if I hadn't forced my way out so quickly.

Ducking my head down against the weather and trying to brush back the soaking wet hair from my face, I slowly pushed my way to the front of the car. There was a small tree and a rusty old car door, of all things, blocking our way. I was so determined in my task that I hardly noticed the cold. Without a second thought, I wrenched the tree up with all my might and backed my way across the road, dragging it carefully. There were broken off branches, resulting in deadly wooden skewers all up and down the tree. One wrong step, a tumble, and visions of me spiked on a wooden skewer and bleeding to death right there in the road flashed in my mind. So, I treaded carefully. When I reached the side of the road, I laid the tree down gently and went back for the car door, which was surprisingly heavy. I dragged it slowly out of the way, just enough for me to drive around it.

It was then that I noticed I was shivering and ran back to the car. No one else had thought to bring a jacket either. We had been in such a hurry to get going that it hadn't crossed our minds to dress warmer. As I jumped back in I reached over and turned the heater dial up to the highest position, hoping for a quick blast of heat. It worked. A few minutes later we were very toasty, even though I continued shivering. I was no longer cold, just scared to death that we wouldn't reach our destination in time to save her.

About fifteen minutes later, a large tree branch, or perhaps it was the entire tree, flew into us and hit the driver's side of the car with such a loud bang that I jumped and temporarily lost control and skidded sideways. As I frantically hit the breaks and turned the steering wheel into the slide, I started to regain my composure as I saw the tree fly over us, continuing its journey into the darkness of the night. I was able to get us going back in the right direction and continued along. I was so happy at that moment that I had slowed the car down to not much more than a crawl just a few moments before.

"Watch where you are going, Abigail. Are you trying to kill us?" My passenger in the backseat yelled over the storm. That was the first thing she had said during the entire ride. She was bleeding and in a lot of pain, so had only been moaning up until this point.

I was by far the youngest person in the car, but at that moment, I was in charge, and I was in no mood. "Shut the hell up!" I yelled back. "I need to concentrate."

I heard a loud huff from the back seat and not another word was said. Oh boy, was I ever going to pay for that later. But, at the moment I didn't care. I needed to get us to the hospital in one piece.

I continued driving for another few minutes, more nervous than ever. The storm was not letting up, but I was determined to get through it, to fight the forces of nature, and to win. Nothing else on earth mattered at that moment. When we reached the narrow bridge that crossed over the river, I could see that the water was very high and raging wildly. It was actually overflowing the banks and threatening the bridge itself. I didn't know how this was even possible. How long had it been raining? Certainly not long enough for this to happen. But, there it was, right in front of me, very close and threatening.

While crossing the bridge, it suddenly felt like we hit a patch of ice, which was impossible, because it was a summer storm. But that's what it felt like. I had the steering wheel in a death grip. The car started skidding and there was not much I could do about it. I took my foot off the gas and turned into the skid, knowing that was what I was supposed to do, but it wasn't helping. The car seemed to have a mind of its own. I could see, and feel, the bridge railing coming straight for us. For a moment I wasn't sure if we were skidding toward the railing or if it had broken loose and was flying toward us. It felt like it was all happening in slow motion.

I was just sixteen years old and had only practiced driving a couple of times ever. Now here I was, driving the two people I probably hated the most to the hospital, in a horrible storm, and their lives depended on it. But, before I tell you that story, you need to know how we got here.

CHAPTER 2

ONE YEAR EARLIER

Bam! Something, or someone actually, hit me head-on in the hallway of the high school. We both fell to the ground, with books and binders scattering everywhere.

"Watch where you're going, stupid," the other girl screeched at me while I was trying to get up. When I glanced over at her, she didn't even look my way.

As the other girl was getting up, brushing herself off and gathering her things, I started heading down the hallway toward my classroom.

Even though we made quite a commotion, it seemed like no one in the hall noticed. Barely a sideways glance from anyone, as we went on our way to class. I looked over my shoulder as the bell rung and saw the other girl quickly running down the hall in the opposite direction.

A couple of minutes later, she walked into my classroom, out of breath, with an attitude already starting. It was pretty obvious. She stood at the front of the room with her arms crossed and rolled her eyes when she saw me. Every head turned her way. She looked around the room and turned bright red. Then she actually put her left hand up to feel her face, like maybe she had warts all over her, by the way everyone was staring. Then I saw relief flood over her as she realized she was being ridiculous. She looked fine. A little rough around the edges perhaps, but fairly normal either way.

She was actually a very pretty girl, but I'll bet she never really realized it. She looked like she spent all of her time dying her hair, getting body piercings and tattoos, and finding the weirdest, skimpiest clothes she could find. She was the type that would always say she wanted to 'express herself.' To the trained professional she just wanted attention, no matter how much she denied it. She definitely craved male attention. However, with the way she looked, she got the wrong kind of attention. Girls thought she looked ridiculous and hated her, and boys just wanted to sleep with her. No one really took her seriously.

The second the girl walked into the classroom, and was done scrutinizing her face for warts, she looked directly at me again. I turned my head, trying not to be recognized by her. But it didn't work. She had already seen me.

"Hi, you must be Josie," the teacher said as she walked toward her.

"Sorry, I got lost," she said.

"It's okay. Please have a seat." She motioned to an empty desk next to me. The girl looked directly at me and smiled as she walked over and sat down. Just great.

"What's your problem anyway?" Josie whispered to me when the teacher wasn't looking.

I quickly turned away.

"Hey, I'm talking to you," she said more loudly. Everyone in the room turned to look at her. "What?!" She hissed at them. This made everyone turn away from her. They weren't used to being outwardly challenged like that.

Class that day felt like it was never ending and almost unbearable, because Josie wouldn't leave me alone. But, when it did finally end, she was almost the last one out the door. She was waiting for me to leave, so she could get me alone.

"Hey Mousy, I asked you before what your problem was," she said bluntly to me.

"Just leave me alone. And don't call me that."

"Well, what is your name? I'm sure you have one." Josie was not going to let it go.

"Abbey. My name is Abbey. Now will you just leave me alone?" And with that, I raced out the door to my next class. I wasn't afraid of her. She just wasn't worth the hassle. I tried my best to stay out of trouble at school and she looked like a lot of trouble to me. She wasn't the type of person I would ever be friends with.

I didn't see Josie again for the rest of the day, which was just fine with me. After school I walked home alone, like I did every day.

While walking home I thought about Josie. She was pretty, I could tell. She hid most of it with that ridiculous blue hair and the tattoos, but she was definitely pretty. Me? Not so much. I was not what anyone would call beautiful. Certainly not ugly, but just average looking. Average height, with short, bland, sandy colored hair. I did have beautiful blue eyes though. People would remark to me about them all the time. Otherwise, just average. At almost fifteen years old, I was a sophomore in high school, had a few friends at school, but mostly kept to myself. I never really felt like I fit in. I was a good student, probably because I didn't spend a lot of time hanging out with other kids.

Doing my best to avoid Josie after that, I would duck into the bathroom if I saw her walking toward me in the hallway, or hide, feet up, in a bathroom stall if Josie came in after me. She never noticed. Pretty pathetic, I know.

A few days after the hallway collision incident, my luck ran out. I was standing at my locker, with my back facing the crowded hallway, when I suddenly felt a chill run up my spine. I spun around to see what it was that caused it. I was half expecting to see some of the boys with a bucket that moments ago held ice cold water. That's how unnerving the chill up my spine felt. Unfortunately, what I actually found was Josie standing right behind me, only inches from my face. I instantly turned my back to her and slammed my locker shut, wanting to get out of there as fast as I could.

"Why are you avoiding me?" Josie asked.

I hesitated for just a moment, staring directly into the closed locker door, then decided that I couldn't really avoid her forever. I was going to have to talk to her sooner or later. I spun around to face her.

"Look, I'm not avoiding you. I just want to go to class. Okay?" I said a bit meekly, looking down at my feet.

"No, not okay. Stop being such a bitch," Josie

responded.

I was not the confrontational kind. This was something that Josie figured out pretty quickly. She knew that she could intimidate me, and actually found it kind of fun.

I then looked up, face to face, staring directly into her eyes. "You are the one being a bitch." I surprised myself by saying that. It just jumped out before I had a chance to think about the consequences. "I gotta go." I said, and headed to my next class quickly. I dared not turn around for fear that I would find Josie hot on my trail.

After school that same day, I was walking home alone, as usual, deep in thought. At one point, Josie came up behind me. She could be really stealthy when she wanted to be.

"Hey Mousy. Whatcha doin'?"

I jumped, because I had no idea that anyone was behind me, causing me to drop my books all over the sidewalk. As I scrambled for them, I kicked one of them into the street. As Josie jumped off the curb to fetch the wayward book, I picked up the rest of them.

"Please just leave me alone," was all that I could muster.

"I'm not here to harass you. In fact, I'm going to let that 'bitch' comment from earlier go."

"What are you talking about? You said it first," was my response, instantly regretting it.

Josie just smiled. "Look, Mousy, we live on the same street. Maybe we can hang out sometime?"

"Stop calling me Mousy. I don't like it." I turned away and continued walking toward home. Josie followed. I hadn't even realized that she lived so close by. I have no idea how she knew where I lived.

I tried my best to ignore her, to no avail, even turning back a couple of times, but Josie was always there right behind me, smiling. It was unnerving. Finally, I saw her turn up a walkway toward the front door of her house. She really did live close to me. Just my luck.

"Bye, Mousy. See you tomorrow," she called out after me, while waving good-bye. I ignored her.

I couldn't quite figure out if Josie was being antagonistic toward me or was genuinely trying to make friends. It didn't matter either way, I wanted nothing to do with her, and didn't mention her to my parents. They weren't snobs at all, but I knew they would say Josie was from the wrong side of the tracks. Did that make them snobs? I wondered. I didn't think so. It didn't really matter, because they didn't seem to understand anything in my life. They didn't understand why I was such a loner and had a hard time making friends. I'm sure some of it had to do with the fact that I was an only child. My parents were very old fashioned, so I didn't tell them much. They didn't really seem to notice.

My father, Leland Harris, was a large man, over six feet tall and broad shouldered. I thought he had a kind face. He intimidated most people, but, really was a sweetheart at home. Maybe a bit strict, but we adored him. He ran a big construction company and didn't make many friends doing it. It went with the territory and he was okay with that.

Rosemary, my mother, was the polar opposite of my father. In her late 30s, she was striking, with bright, distinctive blue eyes. She turned heads everywhere she went. I adored my mother, but always felt overshadowed by her when we went places together. No one ever seemed to notice that I was there. It was all about my mother. I learned early on that being beautiful would make your life much easier, and realized that was probably not going to happen for me.

We lived in a trailer park in a small, rural Maine town. It was a nice neighborhood, as far as trailer parks go, but I have to admit that I was a bit embarrassed by it. I knew the reputation that trailer parks got and didn't need anything else to draw attention to me. This was one of the reasons I almost never brought friends home. My parents asked me about it occasionally, but I just made up some story about going to someone's house and they let it go. In actuality, I would go to the library and bury my nose in a new novel. When sufficient time passed, I would go home. This way, it appeared to them that I had friends, even though they rarely met any of them. I don't know why I felt it necessary to deceive my parents, but I did it anyway. I didn't want them to think of me as a loser.

A few days later, on Saturday, I had nothing better to do, so I was just sitting in the backyard reading a book and taking in some sunshine, when I heard the doorbell ring. I thought nothing of it, figuring it was for my mother. It always was.

"Abbey, you have a visitor," my mother called from inside the house.

Just then, Josie stepped out through the living room sliding door and into the warm backyard sunshine. I had to shield my eyes to see who it was. Recognition then washed over my face and I couldn't hide my disappointment. She was wearing skimpy shorts and a short top, showing off her belly ring. I bet my mom loved that. What in the world was she doing at my house?

"What, not happy to see me?" Josie asked me, smiling.

Josie had newly dyed blue hair and a pierced lip. Even though I could not see my mother, I knew the look she must have had on her face right then.

"What do you want?" I was tired of the cat and mouse game Josie was playing. I put a bookmark in and laid my book down next to me on my chair.

Josie sat down in the other chair and pulled up the legs of her shorts a couple more inches to try and get some color on them. When she did so, there was a distinctive tattoo of a red lizard on her upper thigh. I saw it and immediately turned my head away. When Josie looked up, she was smiling. She liked that she got a reaction out of me, even if it was negative. That was fine with her.

"I just want to hang out, Mousey. Is that okay with you?" It didn't sound rude at all. Josie actually sounded sincere.

"I guess. Why do you keep calling me Mousey? I

don't get it." I really was perplexed.

"Because that is what you are. You're just kind of normal looking, plain, boring and mousey. Sorry, but that's just the way I see it."

That hurt my feelings some, but she wasn't wrong.

"I'm confused. Just days ago we were calling each other names in the hallway at school. Now we're hanging out. That's weird," I told her.

"I know. I'm weird sometimes. So, what do you do for fun in this town? It seems really boring. I thought maybe we could liven things up around here." Josie changed the subject.

"Nothing really. See movies. I don't know."

Josie was right, it was really boring living in a small town. She dreamed of fun and adventure, with lots of fun things to do. No, not in this town.

"Well, I met some people the other day that are having a party tonight. You should come with me. It will be fun." Josie was excited.

"I'm not really the partying kind and I normally stay home on Saturdays. I usually just watch TV or read."

"Yeah, that's what I pretty much figured. Boring." It was subtle, but I saw her eyes roll heavenward.

"My parents will never let me go to a party. They are kinda strict."

"Don't tell them then. Tell them you are coming over to spend the night with me," Josie replied.

"I don't know. I'm not going to know anyone at the party, I'm sure." I was really hesitant.

"That's how you meet people and make friends. Go to parties, mingle, meet cute boys, whatever. Besides, I live just down the street, so you can go home whenever you want. You don't have to spend the night if you don't want to. You can always tell your parents that you got sick or something and just go home after the party." Josie had an answer for everything.

Against my better judgment, I said yes. But, only agreed to go if we could stay for no more than one hour. That would be more than enough for me. Josie agreed.

"Okay, come by my house around eight. You know where I live. We can walk from there. It isn't far," she called as she walked around the corner of the house and out the side gate. I didn't even have a chance to respond.

CHAPTER 3

A few hours later when we arrived at the party, we were both surprised. It was huge. And it was loud. There must have been over 300 people there. The house was a mansion, with a huge game room and an olympic sized swimming pool. I didn't even know there were any houses that large and fancy in my part of town. It looked to me like half the people at the party were in the pool. Some had clothes on, some didn't. There was not an adult anywhere that I could see. I wondered who the house belonged to and why they were allowing the party to happen. I realized then that the parents must be out of town and someone, among the hundreds there, must be their kid. He or she was having a huge bash, at their parents' expense.

I couldn't imagine ever doing something like that to my parents. It wasn't right. I knew that I was way too much of a good girl, by the standard of most teenagers, but I didn't care. I had no desire whatsoever to act like they did. I got made fun of by the kids I went to school with because I was such a nice girl. Whatever. I wasn't going to change myself to please them. As a result, I spent a lot of time alone. That's why I agreed to go to the party in the first place. I thought it wouldn't kill me to get out and socialize a bit.

Before I realized that she was gone, Josie left me standing in the middle of the back patio all by myself. Then one of the boys, really cute and wearing nothing but a pair of powder blue swim trunks, seemed to come from nowhere and handed me a red cup with beer in it. I tried to give it back, but he disappeared into the crowd, as quickly and mysteriously as he had appeared. Josie walked up with a drink in her hand and noticed my reaction to the party, and the beer.

"You don't drink beer?" she asked me.

"Well, I've tried it, but don't like it."

Josie looked around to make sure no one was watching us. "Let's try something else, then," she whispered to me.

"Like what? I can't go home drunk."

"No, not booze. Follow me." Josie took my red cup from me, sat it and her drink down on the living room table and started heading down a long hall, motioning for me to follow her. She then opened the door to some room at the very end of the hall. She stuck her head in and looked around, before opening the door wide enough for us both to enter. "This will do," she said, as I followed her into the room, curious. She closed the door behind me.

"What will do?" I asked her, looking around at the empty room. It was obviously a pre-teen girl's bedroom. It was decorated in pink and had posters on the wall of the latest teen heartthrobs. It made me a little uneasy.

"You'll see." Josie pulled some items out of her purse and laid them on the dresser. "Lock the door, will you." She didn't even look up at me.

"Is that cocaine?" I asked, eyes wide, as I reached over and locked the bedroom door.

"Yes, you ever try it before?" Josie knew this was a dumb question.

"No, and I'm not going to now."

"Just a little. It's not gonna kill you. Don't be such a nerd." Josie taunted me. 'Nerd' was a word people didn't really use anymore, but Josie thought it was appropriate, and she didn't like sounding like everyone else.

"I said no."

As I headed toward the bedroom door, Josie caught me by the left arm and turned me toward her. It happened so fast that I didn't even have time to react.

"Really? You are afraid to just try a little? I do it all the time and I'm fine. Come on, you can't be so afraid of everything in your life. Live a little." She gave me a 'come on, you can do it' look.

I wasn't stupid and knew this was peer pressure at its finest, but felt that Josie had a point. Was I going to spend the rest of my life scared? A little bit wasn't going to hurt me. "I don't know," was all I could say.

During the couple of minutes that we debated whether I was going to try it or not, Josie had made a few lines of cocaine on a mirror she had brought with her. She never left home without it, I found out later.

"Look, just try one. I'll show you how." With that, Josie bent over and snorted one line. It looked really easy. She smiled when done and handed over the straw to me. "Well?" She waited for an answer, as she wiped excess powder off her nose with her sleeve.

I found myself reaching for the straw without really

meaning to. "Well, okay. Just one." And I meant it. I bent over and tentatively snorted one line. It gave me a rush like I had never felt before. "Oh, wow," was all I could say.

That made Josie smile.

After that night, it didn't take long before partying was a frequent event in our lives. I knew it was wrong, but couldn't help myself. I just got caught up in it all. We did cocaine and drank frequently. Drugs and alcohol brought me out of my shell and I started making new friends. I really liked that I wasn't the one holding up the wall at gatherings anymore. When I was high, I could say and do anything. It didn't matter what the consequences were, and my friends thought I was hilarious. These were friends that my parents disapproved of, and I didn't care.

I even started to look like Josie. I dyed my hair black and started dressing all in black. I even got a couple of tattoos that my parents didn't know about, but I showed them off freely at school. After a few weeks, we started skipping a lot of school, so we could go get high with our friends. It all happened so fast that I didn't even realize what a stupid thing I was doing with my life.

It didn't take long until we ran out of friends that would give us free stuff. We were too young to have jobs to pay for our fun activities, so we started stealing. We would take a couple of things here and there from the houses where the parties were held. But, we knew that was risky and needed to find other ways. If we got caught, we would never be invited anywhere again.

One day, we were hanging out at my house, watching TV. Josie had just dyed the tips of her blue hair to a bright pink. It was sure to catch the attention of everyone who saw her. Though if you ask her, that was not her intention at all. She just wanted to be herself. Sure she did.

"This is so boring. Let's get high," Josie whispered. She didn't want my mother to hear her.

"We don't have any money. How do you think we are going to get high?" I whispered back.

"Well..." Josie tilted her head toward the dining room table, never losing eye contact with me. I turned to see what she was motioning toward.

"No way. I'm not stealing money from my mother's purse!" I said a little too loudly.

"Shhh. Do you want her to hear you?" Josie whispered at me with wide eyes, staring right into mine. "Come on, just a few dollars. That's all. She'll never miss it. In my experience, moms never know exactly how much money is in their purse. She'll never even know. If she didn't trust you or was suspicious in any way, she would never leave her purse out, especially with the likes of me hanging around." She burst out laughing. I couldn't help but smile.

"I'll do it. You don't even have to. Go in the kitchen and distract your mother. You won't even be the guilty one. I will." Josie got up and started walking toward the dining room table and waved her hand at me to go into the kitchen. "Go on," she whispered.

It looked to me like Josie was going to do it

whether I helped or not, and I didn't want her to get caught. I liked Josie and didn't want to be banned from seeing her. So, I got up and went into the kitchen and made small talk with my mother. About 30 seconds later, I looked toward the living room and Josie was sitting on the couch trying to get my attention. That was really fast. Oh good, she chickened out.

I went into the living room and sat next to Josie. "Why didn't you do it?" I asked Josie.

"Who said I didn't? This isn't my first rodeo, you know. Let's go." She jumped up and headed toward the front door.

I obediently followed her. "I'll be back later, Mom," I called into the kitchen as we darted out the front door.

CHAPTER 4

A few days later, on a Tuesday after school, I walked into the house and both of my parents were sitting at the dining room table looking at me. They had judgment written all over their faces. It was very strange. My father was never home so early in the day. Something was definitely up.

"What?" I asked as I headed toward the kitchen for a snack.

"Please come in here and sit down," my father said sternly.

I turned to look at him, a bit confused.

"Can I get a snack first?"

"No," he responded. "We need to talk to you."

I could tell that he was serious and I walked over and sat down at the table across from my parents.

"What's going on?" I asked, a bit worried. Overall, my parents were pretty easy going. But they looked serious.

"Abbey, we are very worried about you," my mother started.

I looked back and forth between my parents, who looked deadly serious. "What do you mean?"

"We know about the drugs," my father said.

Oh boy. What am I going to do now? I quickly decided to play stupid, as teenagers often do, and gave them a quizzical look. "What drugs?"

It didn't take long to become abundantly clear that my act was not going to work on them. They proceeded to tell me how they had been talking to my friends' parents who told them that Josie and I had come over to their houses many times high on something. They let it go a couple of times, but decided that it was time to tell my parents about their daughter. They apparently told Josie's parents also. My father said he didn't know the outcome of that conversation.

"We also know that you've been skipping school. Abbey, you've always been a really good student. What is going on with you?" he asked me.

"They're lying!" I yelled at my parents as I started to get up.

There was no way I could admit to them what I was doing. I was so ashamed. None of that behavior was like me at all. At least it didn't used to be.

"Sit down!" my father said in a voice that I had never heard before. It made me jump and I sat down promptly.

"We've noticed a changed in your behavior also. We just didn't realize it was drugs. Now we know and we are really worried about you," he said, a little softer this time.

"Dad, it's not true," I tried convincing him. My mother just sat there with a disapproving look on her face. Somehow that was worse than being yelled at.

"We are thinking of putting you in rehab," my father told me.

"What? No! I don't need rehab. Dad, I don't have a problem. You don't know what you're talking about!" With that, I ran into my room and slammed the door.

They didn't follow.

Late that night I made a rash decision, one that would change the entire course of my life. I wish now that I could take it all back. You know what they say about hindsight. I packed up a few of my belongings, took all the cash my mother had in her purse, and walked out the front door. There was no way I was going into rehab. It was ridiculous, I wasn't an addict. We were just having fun, that was all.

It was a beautiful, clear night with a billion stars out. I walked to Josie's house down the street with just the moonlight guiding my way and knocked softly on her window. She opened it a minute later.

"What are you doing here in the middle of the night?" a sleepy Josie asked me, while rubbing the fog from her eyes. Her blue hair was wilder than usual, sticking up everywhere. She had washed off all of the dark makeup she usually wore, and was actually pretty with just her bare face. I barely recognized her.

"My parents want to put me in rehab. What am I going to do?" I wailed.

"Shhh, you'll wake my mom and dad. Come in." Josie stepped aside while I climbed through the open window.

I spent the next several minutes telling her all about the fight I had with my parents, embellishing my part in it, to make myself sound way tougher than I actually was with my parents. I couldn't help myself. For some reason I found it necessary to always make myself sound better to Josie than I really was. I'm not sure if she was fooled or not. She said she was sorry all of that happened, but what could she do?

"Aren't you going to help me?" I asked her, unsure why I even had to ask. Josie was my best friend. Why wouldn't she want to help? "Did your parents get mad when they found out about the drugs?"

"They don't care. They never have. They just told me to be careful and that was that. But, I can't let you stay here. My parents would never allow that. I'm sorry." Josie really did seem to feel sorry. Her parents didn't really pay much attention to her, but they wouldn't let one of her friends crash there, that she was sure of. "You can stay tonight, but you have to leave very early, before they wake up," she told me.

"Are you freaking kidding me? This is all your fault. You are the one that got me taking drugs, stealing from my parents and other people, and got me into this. Now you aren't going to do anything? You're just going to abandon me?" I was furious. It was a side of me that I hadn't really seen before. I didn't know I had it in me.

"Just get out," Josie said calmly, pointing toward the window.

"Never mind! I don't need your help," I yelled.

At that point, I didn't care if I woke up anyone else in the house. I crawled out the window and dropped clumsily to the ground. Josie slammed it quickly behind me, almost catching my fingers in it. I glared at her and walked away into the darkness, as I saw her bedroom light go out. I wondered why I had ever hung out with her at all. She obviously didn't care what happened to me. She was all about Josie.

Now what was I going to do? I couldn't go back home after making such a spectacle of myself and storming out like that. Luckily it was a nice night, and I just wandered around until daylight, trying to figure out my next move.

I hadn't thought any of it through. I ended up spending the next two days sleeping in unlocked cars. I used up the few dollars I had on drugs and ran out of money pretty quickly. I had almost no food and had no choice but to go back home. I was starving.

When I arrived home, my parents were so happy to have me back, that they temporarily forgot the reason I left in the first place. Even though it had been only a couple of days, my mother said I looked skinny and made me a sandwich. I scarfed it down like I had never eaten before, which is exactly what it felt like. I was so hungry, I couldn't eat it fast enough. My mother saw how hungry I was and made me another sandwich, which I ate almost as fast.

For several days, no one mentioned drugs, rehab, or the fact that I had stolen all of the money out of my mother's wallet when I left. Because they were so happy to have me back, I sensed that they were afraid to ruin it.

I took some time to think about what I was doing and realized that my life was in a downward spiral. So I decided to try and straighten up. I went back to school and tried to get off the drugs. That part wasn't so easy for me. I felt like I needed the drugs to cope with life. Was I addicted? I didn't want to admit it, but I probably was.

"Whatcha doin'?" Josie came up to me a few days after starting back to school.

"Nothing," I said, still angry with Josie for not helping me. But I did miss having a friend.

"Let's hang out after school," Josie said. "I'll meet you in the parking lot." She walked away before I had a chance to say no.

Over the next few weeks, I went back to my same old ways with Josie. We frequently got high and missed a lot of school. And, I started fighting a lot with my parents. They tried to reign me in, but it wasn't working. They just didn't understand me. After about the hundredth fight, I had had enough. One morning, I grabbed my things and left the house for school, and never went back.

I didn't even go to Josie this time. Josie wouldn't care. She lived in her own little world, and if it didn't affect her, then there was no point in bothering her about it. I knew my parents would be devastated when I didn't return home, with no note or call or anything. At that point, the drugs had such a strong hold on me that I just didn't care. I didn't care about anything or anyone.

I hitchhiked my way south to New York City and I spent weeks sleeping in empty cars and buildings, and foraging for food. I got odd jobs here and there doing yard work, even cleaning houses, but none of it lasted. I even broke into empty houses and cars and stole anything I thought I could sell. Then I spent all of my money on drugs, I just couldn't help it. It was more important to me to be high, than to have food. I started to get really skinny and sick all the time. I knew that I couldn't continue to live like that. It was a reckless way to live and it would kill me eventually.

I managed to get myself arrested a couple of times on petty theft and drug charges, and even spent my 15th birthday in jail. How sad is that? Luckily, there were no witnesses and no proof and they couldn't hold me. They didn't even know my real name and thought I was eighteen, so had no reason to call my parents.

One night while sleeping in an abandoned house, I woke up with a start as someone jumped on me. I never saw a weapon, but I fought fiercely for my life anyway, not really knowing what his true intentions were. Somehow I broke free from him and I ran out into the night, grabbing my duffel bag on my way out.

I knew I was extremely lucky that I got away, and it was the scariest thing that had ever happened to me. It took a while, but I eventually saw myself for what I was, a homeless drug addict. I knew that if I didn't do something about it immediately, I might not be so lucky next time. If I didn't die at the hands of some other homeless person, then I would probably die from the drugs, or even starvation. I was in a desperate way and needed to find another way to survive.

With the help of a woman I met that worked at a homeless shelter I was able to get into rehab. It's ironic that if I had just stayed home and gone into rehab when my parents wanted me to, I wouldn't be in the mess I was currently in. The facility was run by the state and was free, which is the only way I was going to get in. I didn't have a penny to my name and knew I wouldn't last one more day out in the world.

Rehab was the hardest thing I have ever done in my life. During the first few days, I just knew I was going to die. Then something wonderful happened. The fog lifted, I started feeling better and was clear headed for the first time in months. Oh, I still wanted to get high, but I had people that helped me with that and I knew that I would make it through. After about a month in the facility, it was time for me to leave. The woman from the shelter came to visit me and gave me some money to get started. It wasn't much at all, but at least I would not starve while I looked for a job.

CHAPTER 5

Having decided that I needed to get out of the big city, and try to make a life elsewhere, I made my way to a small town called Ashford, in Maine. It was near the coast and the cutest town I have ever seen. I looked for a job for a few days and had no luck. I was a bit scruffy from my time on the streets. Most people took one look at me and all of a sudden the job was filled. I guess that's my own fault.

I made friends, well sort of, with a young man that worked at a local restaurant. I would stand outside of it during the day, hoping someone would buy me a meal, which they did occasionally. I think he felt sorry for me.

One day he walked up to chat as usual during his lunch break. He brought me a burger that someone said was too well done and had sent back. I didn't care. I was so hungry. As I wolfed it down, he started talking.

"Are you looking for a job?" he asked me.

"Yes. I need one badly," I said with my mouth full.

"Well, I know someone that works at the horse breeding farm outside of town and he said they are looking for a cook's assistant. I guess theirs just quit. Can you cook?"

"I'm actually a pretty good cook. Where do I apply?"

"I don't know. It's at the Tyler Estate. I guess you could just go out there."

He proceeded to give me directions while I finished my burger. I thanked him and started walking. I realized then that I never did ask him his name. I would have to find that out later.

About 45 minutes later I reached the estate. It was a beautiful sunny day and I didn't mind walking. I was a bit sweaty by the time I arrived though. I have to say that I was amazed. It was the most impressive house I have ever seen. It had a tree lined driveway that seemed to stretch for miles, and the house was huge. I have never seen one so large. It was on a huge ranch with a lot of horses and people working there. A few of the ranch hands looked at me strangely as I walked up to the house, but that didn't matter. This was probably my last shot at survival.

As I walked up to the circular driveway heading to the front door, it suddenly opened. A young couple walked out, followed by an older gentleman. He was probably an employee by the looks of him. He looked about 60 years old, but was well over six feet tall and a bit more than 200 pounds. He had dark eyes and dark hair, that was just starting to gray at the temples. Even at his age, he was an imposing man. I wondered if he was their body guard.

"How many servants do we have? Two? And I'm expected to do everything else?" the woman wailed at what looked to be her husband, as they walked toward their car. The older gentleman walked around them and opened the back door for them.

"You know we have a lot more than two people working here, Sarah," He replied.

The woman was in her 20s. I would say she was pretty, certainly not beautiful. She had short, brunette hair and in the few seconds that I observed her, she seemed to have an air about her that said she was not really that friendly, like she was better than everyone else.

Just then, they noticed me. They both stopped and looked at me curiously.

"Can we help you?" the woman called Sarah asked me. She looked me up and down and obviously did not like what she saw.

I couldn't really blame her. I walked up wearing faded jeans with a large hole in the left knee, a ratty t-shirt with a picture of Jim Morrison on it, and even rattier tennis shoes. This was almost everything I owned. I knew better than to show up dressed like that, but had no other choice. I had very little makeup on and looked a bit scruffy. I had been living on the streets for a few weeks and obviously didn't look my best. Now that I was off drugs it was time to put my life back together, get a job and become a productive human being. I knew this was what I wanted, even at 15 years old.

"Hi," I said, feeling a little shy, and way underdressed. I never imagined that they would see me right on the spot. I wasn't prepared for an interview, and certainly wasn't dressed for one. Not that it would have made any difference. My other clothes were no better. "A guy I met in town said you were looking for a cook." I looked down at my feet.

As I looked back up, Sarah gave me a look of

disapproval, so her husband stepped in.

"Hello," he said, reaching out to shake my hand. "I'm Adam Tyler and this is my wife, Sarah," he told me, motioning toward her.

"Hi," I said again, and looked over at Sarah. "I'm really sorry I'm dressed this way," looking down at my worn clothing and brushing imaginary things off of my shirt while talking. "I didn't think I would be meeting you right now. But, I could really use a job. I'm a good cook."

"Who in the world shows up at the door unannounced?" Sarah asked. She obviously didn't care that I was standing right there.

Adam just shrugged his shoulders without even looking her way.

"Maybe I should come back later," I said, turning to leave.

"It's perfectly all right," Adam told me. I don't know why, but he seemed to like me, or at least was just a nice person. "What is your name?"

"Abigail. Well..Abbey." I stuttered, nervously.

"Abigail, we have a few minutes before we have to leave. Why don't you come in and sit down. We can have a talk." He motioned toward the door, and the doorman, or whatever he was, walked around us toward the front door.

"It's Abbey. No one calls me Abigail," I said shyly, noticing how cute Adam Tyler was. He was tall, and not much older than I was. He had sandy colored hair and the most beautiful green eyes I have ever seen. I knew immediately that I had better keep my distance from him.

"Okay, Abbey then," he responded, and smiled my way. I think he could tell I was very nervous and he wanted to make me feel a little more comfortable. I smiled shyly back.

"Well this is very out of the ordinary. We usually go through the employment service in town," Sarah said, looking at both of us.

"Sorry," I said and again turned to leave. This woman was not giving me a job today.

"Wait," Adam called after me. Sarah and I both stopped in our tracks and turned to face Adam.

"You just said that we need more help around here. Why don't you at least talk to her? It can't hurt," Adam said to Sarah.

Sarah thought for a moment. This was a woman that really didn't like her routines deviated from. That was obvious from the moment I met her. Perhaps she thought it made her look weak. Even though she herself was only in her twenties, I think she wanted to make sure everyone knew she was not to be messed with. She was in charge.

"I don't know, Adam. How would that look?"

"Look to who? Just talk to the girl already," he responded. It seemed that he liked to keep things simple. "What is the point in going through an agency, when there is someone standing at our door wanting a job? She did say she was a good cook." He looked over at me and smiled again.

Reluctantly, Sarah agreed. "Okay John, show her in." She said to the doorman, without looking at him directly. She flicked her hand at him in a dismissive manner. He opened the door, they entered first, then me, followed by John. They led me to a large, but cozy room.

"Thank you," Adam said, and John disappeared quickly.

Adam motioned to an open chair across from a couch that Sarah sat down on. Then he sat down next to her.

The room was a library. It had floor to ceiling books on every wall. I was mesmerized, but needed to concentrate on the people sitting across from me. I could check it out later, if I got the job.

Up until this point, Sarah hadn't said much. She didn't like the looks of me. I could tell. I was scruffy, I know.

"So, where have you worked before?" Sarah asked me bluntly.

I was a bit startled at Sarah's sudden question, and hesitated a moment while I thought about what I should say. I realized then that I was completely unprepared for an interview. Why in the world did I just show up without trying to dress a bit nicer and at least rehearsing the answers to some questions I might be asked? I probably looked and sounded like an idiot.

"Well?" Sarah was starting to get impatient, and gave Adam a look that said 'Why are we wasting our time with her?'

Adam patted her hand, and gave her a 'just be

patient' look.

They both looked back to me for an answer.

"Well, I have done a lot of odd jobs. Nothing long term, all under the table. I know I really don't have any references, but I really am a good cook and if you just give me a chance, I'll prove it to you." It really wasn't the answer she was expecting, I'm sure. But, it was all I had.

"What is your last name?" Sarah asked. She must have realized that I had only said 'Abigail' when introducing myself.

"Oh, well...it's Hunter." I blurted out. That was the name of an old boyfriend, and the only name I could come up with on the spot. I didn't want them to know my real name. I was a runaway and was afraid that if the cops found out, I would be arrested, because I had some petty theft and minor drug charges against me. Those charges had been dropped, but I didn't know if they could be revived upon me getting arrested for being a runaway or not. So, I lied. I prayed that they wouldn't see right through me.

"How old are you?" Adam asked me.

I knew that if I told them I was 15, they would probably call the cops, or at the very least, kick me to the curb. "I'm 18," I lied. They seemed to believe me.

"Well, the cook's assistant just quit, so we are shorthanded. I don't see any reason why we can't give you a chance to prove that you can cook," Adam told me.

Sarah glared at him. But, I could tell that she didn't want to argue with him in front of anyone. She probably thought it was tacky. So, she let it go for the time being. I had a feeling that they would talk about it later.

"That would be fantastic. Thank you!" I jumped up and grabbed his hand to shake it. When I reached for Sarah's hand, she jerked it back as if I had just bitten her. I knew immediately that I was going to have trouble with the lady of the house.

"When do you want me to start?" I asked. "I have to go find a place to stay first."

"Oh, no, I don't think you understand," Adam replied. "This job comes with a room in the staffs' quarters."

I was shocked. "What? I can move in here? Oh wow. I don't know what to say." I started to tear up. I had been living on the streets so long and couldn't even imagine having my own place to stay, even just a simple room in such a beautiful place.

"Of course," Adam said. "Go get your things. You can start right away."

"Thank you so much!" I turned my head away so they wouldn't see the tears. "I'll go get my things. They are just outside in a duffle bag." I headed for the door.

Adam and Sarah looked at each other, but I dismissed it and headed out to get my things. As soon as I was out of the room, I heard Sarah start talking and decided to stop and listen, because I was sure they were going to talk about me.

"What in the world are you thinking? We don't know this girl and she has no references. All of her possessions are in a duffle bag for god's sake. She could kill us in our sleep. Or worse, rob us blind."

"Seriously, don't be so dramatic," Adam replied. In my mind he rolled his eyes at her. I could just tell from the tone of his voice. If that's actually what happened, Sarah chose to ignore him. "She is just a young girl, down on her luck. She looks like she could use a helping hand. We have plenty of room here and really could use the help. You were just complaining that you have to do everything, weren't you? Besides, I think you made some comment the other day about starving to death if the cook didn't get some help. Let's give her a chance. I'm sure she'll be just fine."

He was so calm about the situation. I knew I was going to like him. Sarah seemed like she couldn't help being worried. I couldn't really blame her. They didn't know me and had no idea what I was capable of.

"I will have John keep a close eye on her. We can't just let her have the run of the place. She is a dirty vagrant after all," I heard Sarah say. I'll bet that she crinkled up her face in disgust when she called me a 'dirty vagrant.'

She had a point though.

I was afraid one of the staff would catch me eavesdropping, so I left quickly to get my things. I had dropped my duffle bag in the bushes right before I came across them in the driveway. When I went back into the house, Adam instructed John to show me to my new room and to introduce me to Oliver, the head cook. Oliver would be thrilled to have help. He had been complaining for weeks about all the work he had to do alone, Adam told me.

John led me through the back hallway to the servants' quarters. The house just seemed to get darker and smaller, the further back we walked. I almost felt like ducking down from the low ceiling as we walked down the dank hallway. It was just a feeling. The ceiling wasn't actually any lower than any other part of the house, it just felt that way. But, I didn't mind. Anything was better than some of the places I had stayed in during my time out in the world.

When we reached my room, I was pleasantly surprised. It was very small, no doubt. Only large enough for one bed and a dresser. But, it was heaven. I would be happy here. A job and a place to live. Right then it felt like I hit the lottery.

CHAPTER 6

Working at "the ranch," that's what everyone called the huge estate we were on, was a dream come true. I was in heaven and had no idea how I got so lucky, after all my questionable decisions over the last few months. I started my days very early, getting everything ready for breakfast. I even started before Oliver, the head cook, arrived at work. It was my job as his assistant to do all of the prep work for the entire day's meals. And boy, there was a lot of it. We had to feed the family, of course, but we also cooked for the entire house staff, as well as all of the ranch hands.

Most of the ranch hands, and their families, lived on the property in one of the many cabins peppered all over the ranch. I have no idea how many there were. Dozens, I'm sure. So, we cooked for everyone. It was an amazingly difficult, and very rewarding job. I couldn't have been happier. I worked from dawn until everyone was fed all three meals, and everything was cleaned up. My days were about fourteen hours long, which was just fine with me. It kept my mind and body occupied and away from the things I needed to stay away from. I did get a few breaks here and there, between meals. When I did get a break, once in a while I would wander out to the stables and talk to Walter. He was one of the ranch hands, probably my father's age, and I loved our chats. He was such a nice man and seemed to have a lot of wisdom. I came to depend on his kindness and advice.

The ranch was in the business of horse breeding

and training. Apparently, they had bred and trained a few big money horses and were very well respected in the horse community. Adam's grandparents started the ranch many years ago and Adam would inherit it one day. In the meantime, he seemed to work very hard at the business. He definitely was not one for sitting by idly and letting the ranch hands do all the work. I frequently saw him outside working with the horses. I wasn't exactly sure what he did, but he seemed to work hard at it.

Though Sarah didn't want to introduce me to anyone, I got to know the ranch staff quite well, since I fed them every day. Sarah didn't introduce any of the staff to anyone. I think we were beneath her. It seemed like she felt she was better than the rest of us. She was somewhat nice to me, though I'm sure we would never be friends. She told me that Violet said the help should always know their place. Violet was her mother-in-law. I hadn't met her yet.

The ranch was near the coast, actually only a couple of hours from my parents, in a small town called Ashford. I really didn't get to see much of the town, because I worked so much. But, on my days off I rode into town with John and did a lot of window shopping, while he saw to a few errands of his own. He had warmed up to me a bit since I showed up in the driveway that day. But, we would not be best friends anytime soon. Even though he also was an employee of the ranch, it was painfully obvious that he thought of himself as better than the rest of us. This was probably because he was the personal driver for the family and not someone that cleaned out the stables or worked in the kitchen. He told me that he had been working for the Tyler family for almost 40 years and had watched Adam grow up. He seemed to have a lot of respect for Adam Tyler. He rarely mentioned Adam's mother, Violet, and I had a feeling the respect did not extend to her. He was very discreet about it all, certainly not a gossip.

I also spent much of my free time feeding the numerous chickens that just wandered freely around the ranch. It wasn't my job, but I never saw anyone else feeding them, so I took it upon myself to do it. Gathering eggs was fun too. Adam loved fresh eggs and I made them for him almost every morning. I had to get up very early to collect them, but it was well worth it when Adam thanked me for the delicious breakfast. Sarah didn't seem to notice.

In addition to the sprawling ranch, the house itself was something to marvel about. It had three floors, dozens of bedrooms, and a grand winding staircase that was something to behold. I could just picture beautiful rich ladies of the past, in luxurious gowns, delicately descending the stairs along with their dashing companions, enjoying every bit of attention received. I wondered if I would ever descend those stairs, on the arm of a handsome man, on my way to a grand party in the ballroom. No, of course I wouldn't. It wasn't my house, and I would never be invited to one of their fancy parties. I was the help.

From what I could tell no one actually used the second and third floors, everyone's bedrooms were on the first floor. The staff went up each day to dust everything, but that was it. I really couldn't understand why the staff couldn't stay in the bedrooms on the second and third floors, instead of the dark, teeny rooms we were given. Those spacious, elegant rooms were just sitting there unused. I eventually explored all of the bedrooms. Some of them had sitting rooms and the actual bedrooms were at least 1,000 square feet, larger than some entire houses I have been in. Such a waste. I once made the mistake of asking Sarah about the unused floors. She curtly told me that those were reserved for guests and they would stay that way. I never brought it up again.

There was a formal dining room, of course, that could seat 50 people. They only used it when entertaining, which wasn't often. Normally they ate in the smaller dining room. It was definitely more cozy and intimate. The formal dining room was just gorgeous with gold and silver accents, and several beautiful paintings on the walls. The best part of the room was the large picture window that looked out into the garden. Everything, it seemed, was in bloom and it was breathtaking. Even though I'm sure Adam and Sarah probably wouldn't like it if they found out, I usually ate my meals in the formal dining room. No one was ever in there but me, making it nice and serene, with a beautiful view. Besides, no one actually forbid me to use it. I really couldn't understand rich people. They had so much and took it all for granted.

And the ballroom. Where to start? It was a sight to behold, for sure. It could hold hundreds of people and

I'm sure grand, glorious parties had been held in there. None since I had arrived, but I heard the stories. Sarah did like to go on about the parties that Violet threw. Sarah liked to embellish her stories and in her version, she did it all. She was the planner, decorator, hostess, you name it. When she started her stories, Oliver and I gave each other a knowing look. It was all Violet and we knew it. I hadn't even met Violet yet, but she was the one with the reputation for throwing the grandest parties in the state. I really couldn't wait for one to happen. I wanted to see what all the fuss was about.

 I don't think Sarah cared much for me, but she was mostly decent. A snide remark here and there, but I could handle her. We certainly were never friends. I'm sure she thought of me as "the help." Well, that's technically what I was. I couldn't deny that. One day Sarah was telling me about the ranch and when she first saw it, and how she was so enamored with it. I told her that it was my dream one day to have a place like this and she just laughed at me. I was terribly hurt. I wasn't stupid though, I knew it would probably never happen for me.

CHAPTER 7

A few weeks after I started working at the ranch, Adam's mother arrived home. She had been traveling around Europe for a couple of months with a friend. I found out about her right after I started working there. Oliver, the head cook, was a terrible gossip. He yapped about everyone non-stop every single day while we were in the kitchen. I enjoyed it immensely and knew quite a bit about Violet before I ever laid eyes on her.

Violet Tyler was a striking woman. Even now in her 60s, I could see that she was once very beautiful and would still turn heads. I am talking movie star good looks. She was tall and very poised, exactly what you would expect from someone of such wealth and prestige. She had the most beautiful violet eyes I had ever seen. I guess that's where her name came from.

I knew that Violet Tyler owned the championship horse farm, and Adam was in charge of running it. The staff around the ranch could be very gossipy, which, I hate to admit it, was a lot of fun. Their son and daughter-in-law, Sarah, lived there, but weren't technically the owners. Not yet, anyway. Sarah fancied herself the lady of the house though. Violet let some of it go, just to make Adam happy, I'm sure. Though I doubt it was in Violet's nature to worry about getting along with anyone.

Violet doted on Adam. I could tell that he was the one person in the world that she loved the most. He was her only child and she indulged him in anything he wanted. He was an adult and was married, but

Violet sometimes treated him like he was her 10 year old son. She often bought him gifts and talked about him frequently. He was the same way with her, and almost acted like a little boy whenever she was around. Their relationship was near the top of the creepy scale. No, there was nothing sordid going on between them, they just had an odd relationship from what I could see. He was the definition of a mama's boy.

    Henry, Adam's father, died a couple of years before I arrived, so I never had the chance to meet him. Oliver told me that he was the life of the party and everyone loved him. Everyone except Violet. I heard that Violet detested Henry and only stayed with him for his money. That is very sad, when you think about it. No amount of money could ever get me to stay with someone for 30 or 40 years, if I didn't truly love him. What kind of life Violet and Henry must have had together, I wondered.

    Apparently Henry and Violet met when they were in college and were together ever since. Oliver told me that Henry adored Violet and how much he doted on her. None of it mattered to Violet though. She had a long string of affairs during their marriage, and many people speculated that Adam was not even Henry's son. I heard that Henry knew nothing about any of it. It seems unlikely that Violet could pull that off for so many years without him knowing anything. Perhaps he did know and just didn't care? No way to tell at this point.

    Since she was so unhappy with Henry, that might explain her strange relationship with her son. He may have been some sort of surrogate. Adam did appear to be the only person she cared anything about. It seemed to me as if she treated everyone else as replaceable. How sad for her.

Henry's death was suspicious, but that's really all that was said about it. He suddenly became sick and died within a few days. The doctors blamed it on liver disease, from years of hard drinking. I heard that there was no autopsy, because the family didn't want one. I guess when you are rich it's easy to get people to go along with things. I definitely didn't know much about it. Maybe the coroner honestly didn't think it was necessary to do an autopsy. Even though I enjoyed the gossip, I tried to filter out the things that just didn't add up. Henry probably just died from liver disease and that was the end of it. The truth was probably not really all that juicy.

For some reason that I can't explain, Violet hated me, and I had no idea why. It seemed to start the second she arrived home. I don't think I was imagining it. I tried to be nice to her, always smiling and being friendly, but it didn't seem to matter. I did my best not to take it personally, because she was that way with everyone that I could see. She rarely spoke to me, usually just when she wanted me to fetch her things. I hated it, but I did it anyway. I don't think she realized that I was the cook's assistant, not the butler. She spent a lot of time sitting in the parlor drinking tea alone. It seemed that she didn't do much else.

One day, she was sitting in the library, which was odd, because that was where Adam worked. He was usually in there and it was the first time I had ever seen her there without him. She rang the stupid little gold bell that she had to summon the servants and called me in to bring her some tea. When I walked back in with the tea a few minutes later, she was just sitting there staring out the window, and hadn't even noticed me walk in.

She was wearing comfortable cream colored slacks, a nice white blouse, and heels. No matter what, I never saw the woman in anything but nice clothes and shoes, with her hair done impeccably. She had a hair dresser that came to the house every single morning at 7 a.m. sharp to do her hair. I couldn't even imagine her in a pair of sweats, tennis shoes, and a pony tail. The thought made me smile. I quickly looked her way to make sure she didn't see me smile. I wouldn't want to try to explain that.

I continued to stand a few feet away from her waiting for her to notice me. I didn't want to startle her, so I waited patiently for several minutes. She didn't like anyone approaching her without an invitation, she was kind of skittish like that, which is why I didn't walk right up to her with the tea she had asked for. After a few more minutes, it seemed like she was just going to completely ignore me while I stood there forever. Since she still hadn't acknowledged my presence, I decided to speak up.

"Are you all right?" I finally asked her.

She seemed to snap out of it then and barely glanced my way. "Oh yes, I'm fine." Then she turned away from me again.

I sat the tea and some cookies down on the table next to her and turned to leave.

"Abigail."

She always called me that even though I asked her many times to call me Abbey. She seemed to not care, so I gave up and just went with it. She did tell me that she liked the proper name that I was given, and didn't like the 'cute little nickname' people gave me. She said it was silly and frivolous, and that people should always use their proper names. It was the mature thing to do. Regardless, I still liked to be called Abbey.

"Yes ma'am?" I responded.

"Why don't you come and sit down? I would like to talk to you." She gestured to the empty chair near her.

"Okay." I was very confused at that. Other than ordering me around, she never spoke to me. I promptly sat down in the chair on the other side of the table and turned a bit, so I would be facing her.

Before she said anything to me, I watched her take a small bottle of rum out of her purse, I think it was rum anyway, and pour a bit into her tea. She put it back into her purse and turned to me as if nothing had just happened. It wasn't my place to even think anything of what I just witnessed, so I ignored it. It certainly wasn't the first time I had observed her pouring alcohol into her tea, and probably wouldn't be the last time.

"Have you seen Sarah today?" she asked me.

"Yes, just this morning at breakfast, before she went out. I haven't seen her since. Do you want me to see if I can find her for you?" I asked.

"No, that won't be necessary."

That was all she said for a few minutes, staring out the window again. It made me a little uneasy, just sitting there with no one talking.

"Well, if you don't need anything else, I have a few things I need to get done," and I started to get up.

"Abigail, sit down."

I sat.

"Abigail, you know that when I'm gone, Adam will inherit this entire estate."

"Okay." It was the only response I could think of.

"My problem is that he and Sarah have not been able to have any children," she blurted out.

"I didn't know that," I responded.

Oliver had said that he was surprised that there were no little ones running around, as much as Sarah wanted kids. She apparently talked about them all the time. But I don't think Oliver had any idea that they were having trouble making those children. I wasn't about to tell him though. That's all I needed was for the story to circle around and get back to this conversation I was having with Violet. Even though I liked listening to the gossip, I tried my best not to get involved by repeating the things I heard.

"I need an heir." For the first time, Violet turned her head away from the window and looked directly at me.

I immediately felt really uncomfortable with the conversation and no longer wanted to be there. I didn't know where she was going with that, and I didn't want to know. It was the strangest thing for her to say to me. I was the cook's assistant, not a family member. Why in the world would she ever say something like that to me? I needed to get out of there before this very odd conversation went any further.

"I really have to get back to work." I got up and started walking toward the door.

"Abigail!" She didn't quite yell, but it was definitely stern.

I stopped, turned around and walked back to the chair. I promptly sat down. When the lady of the house yells, I knew I'd better listen.

"Adam's father, Henry, made him marry Sarah. Adam is still so young, and our only son, but Henry wanted him to settle down, start a family, and take over the business. I was against it, of course, but he had a point, so I relented. We put Sarah through medical school, you know. She is a brilliant woman, I have to give her that. She got through in half the time it takes most to get through. She is certainly not one of my favorite people, low class for sure." She very quickly paused at that and looked me up and down. I could tell she was comparing me to Sarah and it made me feel like cattle. Such a strange feeling. "But, I knew that as a doctor she would make a suitable wife for our son."

I did know that Sarah had finished medical school, but was still working on her license, which was why she was gone so much.

At that moment, as if right on queue, Sarah walked in. She looked from from Violet to me and back to Violet again, clearly perplexed. I'm sure we were the last two people she ever imagined would be sitting down having a chat. I jumped up immediately, grateful for the diversion, and almost ran out of the room. Neither one said a word to me. I think I actually felt Sarah's eyes boring a hole into my back as I ran out the door.

CHAPTER 8

I tried my best to keep my head down and just do my job. I loved cooking and couldn't have been happier with the way things turned out. I have to admit though that I had a really hard time staying away from the drugs. But, I told myself that I wouldn't go back to that way of life no matter what, and that's what I intended to do. Still, it was tough, especially at night when I lay in my bed, staring at the ceiling. At that moment, I wanted nothing more than to get high. Oh how I wished that I had never met Josie and gotten into partying. My life certainly wasn't perfect, but it was good, before she showed up. I was doing just fine without her. Even though I know I can make my own decisions, I still blamed Josie for everything that happened to me. If we hadn't literally run into each other in the hallway that day at school, I wouldn't be the runaway drug addict that I turned out to be. I would be home, happy, going to school everyday, and just being a normal teenager. Not now though. Now I was living in a house full of strangers and cooking for them, as well as putting up with their problems and attitude toward me. I knew I wouldn't be there forever, so I would have to make the best of it.

I had even asked around the ranch a bit to see if I could get some cocaine, or anything else for that matter. What I got for my efforts was nothing but a lot of strange looks. It seemed that the Tyler family had a very strict policy against that sort of thing, and had fired many people over the years with nothing but suspicions. So, everyone was terrified of even looking like they were involved in drugs. Good jobs like they had were hard to come by, and they knew it.

I really couldn't blame them. Because I started to fear for my job if someone had a big mouth, I let it go and didn't mention it again to anyone. Still, I could feel them whispering about me whenever I was around. None of it helped me make any friends. For the most part, I was a loner on the ranch. It was a sad way to exist and I just hoped that things would improve as I got to know people. There certainly were plenty of them around, with all the ranch hands and horse trainers they had working there. Not to mention that some of them had their families all living on the ranch also.

I felt that the head chef, Oliver, didn't like me much. He let me be in charge of some of the meals here and there, so he could take some time off, but he didn't do that often. He knew that I was a better cook than he was and he probably feared for his job, even though I never gave him any reason to think I was after it. He still gossiped shamelessly, he couldn't help himself, but he watched me carefully. He clearly didn't trust me and it felt like I had eyes on me all the time.

A few days after my strange encounter with Violet in the library, John found me in the kitchen preparing lamb for the night's dinner. Oliver had gone out for some supplies and I was there alone. I looked up when I heard him walk into the room. At his size, he had a very difficult time sneaking up on anyone. He was a little scary. He looked around to make sure no one was there to hear him.

"Abbey, Mrs. Tyler would like to speak with you in her sitting room," he announced. He had a deep, booming voice, that was hard to ignore. Even though he didn't specify which Mrs. Tyler he meant, I knew.

"Okay, let me finish this up and I'll be right there."

"No. She wants to speak to you right now. That can wait." Impatience was clearly intended in his words.

He wasn't usually so harsh, so I figured I'd better listen. I put down the knife and immediately walked over to the kitchen sink to wash my hands. John crossed his arms and was starting to look irritated.

"I can't really go speak with Mrs. Tyler with lamb's blood on my hands, can I?" I sounded a bit defiant. But really, what did he expect?

John did not respond. He just took a deep breath and let it out slowly. It seemed as if he was trying really hard not to yell at me. Sometimes he forgot that I didn't work for him. As soon as I dried my hands, I followed him to her room. He walked briskly and I had to trot to keep up.

"I know where her room is, John," I called after him, trying to catch my breath.

Again, he did not respond. He quietly knocked on her door and announced my presence, then he turned and left, glaring at me as he walked away.

"Come in Abigail," Violet called through the door.

I knew where her room was, but I had never actually been inside. I was not a maid and had absolutely no reason to ever enter her room. When I did walk in, I was shocked. It was the largest bedroom I had ever seen in my life. It was almost as large as the ballroom, with a sitting room and bathroom connected. Even though the two closets were closed, they looked enormous from the outside. Her room was decorated all in violet and white, and was just gorgeous. It suited her.

"Please come in and sit down." She motioned to a chair opposite of the one she was sitting in, and I sat down.

While I waited quietly for her to tell me why she had summoned me, all kinds of crazy things crossed my mind. Before I had a chance to catalog them all, she started speaking.

"Abigail, I would like to continue our conversation from the other day."

"Okay." I had such a way with words. She didn't seem to notice.

"As I said before, Sarah cannot have children. They have tried and she has seen a few doctors and their chances are very slim. Almost non-existent actually." She looked over at me for some sort of reaction.

"I'm not really sure why you are telling me this. It really is none of my business. I'm sure Adam and Sarah would not want me to know all these personal things about them." I was very nervous. Violet always made me that way whenever I was around her.

"Well, I'm making it your business." She seemed a bit perturbed at my response.

"I'm sorry. I didn't mean to be disrespectful. I just don't understand is all." I tried to make her feel a bit more at ease.

"I know you don't. Let me explain." Even from several feet away, I could smell the rum on her breath.

"Since Adam is our only child, the bloodline stops with him if he has no children. I can't possibly let that happen. He must have a child. It is my duty to see that that happens."

I was confused. I had no idea why she was telling me any of this. I'm sure she could see it on my face.

"This is where you come in." She looked me in the eyes to see if I understood. I didn't.

She waited while I sat there thinking about what she said. Then, all of a sudden the realization hit me.

"Are you kidding me!" I yelled. Jumping up out of my seat, knocking over my chair in my haste.

Violet looked at me, then at the fallen chair, then back up at me. I watched her as she rolled her eyes at me and let out a deep breath of exasperation. She didn't even care that I was looking directly at her when she did it.

"Abigail, please sit down," she calmly said.

"No, I don't think so. You are completely out of your mind if you think I'm going to have his baby!" Then I calmed down for a second, afraid that I was completely wrong about her intentions. "That's what you meant, right?" I said a bit meekly.

"Please sit down, so I can explain." She was still very calm about the whole thing.

I put my chair back upright and sat down. "I am not going to be a surrogate for them. Does Sarah even know we are talking?" I asked her, more calmly now.

"My goodness, Abigail, you are dramatic." She smiled. "I do not want you to become a surrogate. Wherever did you get that idea?" She was being deliberately coy with me.

I was confused again. "Then what in the world am I doing here?" I asked her. The whole conversation was making my head hurt.

She took a deep breath. "Yes, I want you to have Adam's baby. But, Adam and Sarah are to know nothing about our arrangement, ever."

"What? I still don't understand. How would I have his baby without them knowing about it?" I decided to play along to find out where she was going with this.

"Well, they would know you are having his baby. They just wouldn't know I was involved." She smiled tentatively at me.

"That makes no sense. Do you want me to be a surrogate or not?"

"No, Abigail, please try to keep up." By the tone of her voice, she was getting irritated with me. "I'll try to get right to the point. I want you to have Adam's baby. You will then give the baby to Adam and Sarah to raise as their own. I will pay you handsomely for your services. It will be a business arrangement, nothing more. And Adam and Sarah can't know anything about our deal."

I can't believe that I didn't run screaming out of that room as fast as I could, but I was genuinely curious at that point. "So, let me see if I got this right." I began. "You don't want me to be a surrogate, so I'm guessing you are suggesting that I sleep with Adam and get pregnant on purpose? Then I have the baby and hand it over to them? And they are going to be completely fine with the whole thing?" I was not asking rhetorical questions. I really wanted to know the answers.

"Yes, that is pretty much what I am saying. And, once it is done, you will never want for money again, ever. I will make sure you get a generous monthly check for the rest of your life."

I'm sure she had no idea I was only 15 years old. I couldn't tell her though, because I told them I was 18 when I was hired. If I told her now, I would lose everything. I really had no idea how to respond. It was crazy, I know, but I told her I would have to think about it.

"That will be fine, Abigail."

That's when I got out of there as quickly as I could, before she came up with anymore crazy ideas. I headed back to the kitchen to finish my dinner preparations. Oliver was there when I arrived and was terribly upset with me.

"Where the hell have you been? I came back from the store and you weren't here and everything was just sitting out in the open, with no one doing any cooking. Is this what you do every time I leave the house?" he snarled at me.

Oliver was a relatively short man, maybe 5' 8" or so, in his 40s, a bit pudgy, and had long, dark hair. He almost always had it braided down his back. I don't know why he kept it that way. He could actually be handsome if he cut it all off. That day, he had it all piled up on top of his head in a sort of man bun. He looked ridiculous and I fought hard not to laugh at him.

"Of course not. But, Mrs. Tyler, Violet, not Sarah, called me to do some work for her. I couldn't really tell her no." He looked like he didn't believe me. "Go ask her, if you want." I challenged him, pointing in the direction of her room. I knew he wouldn't dare.

Oliver just gave me a look. "Well, get back to work. We are way behind and I am the one that will get admonished if dinner is late," he hissed at me.

I didn't respond. I just finished my work.

CHAPTER 9

After dinner and clean up was all done, I went to my room. I had tried to make my tiny room more homey, because it was terribly plain when I arrived. But, truth is, I didn't have many possessions at all, and certainly nothing to decorate with. Now that I was working steadily, I was saving most of my money, because I didn't need to spend it on much. I had a free place to live, free meals, no expenses for utilities and such. The only thing I spent money on was clothes and a few personal items. None of that came to much, so I saved the vast majority of the money I made.

I didn't want to spend any money on decor for a room in a house that I didn't even own, so I kept my eyes open for things I could use to spruce the place up. I found a few trinkets and framed pictures in the storage room one day and asked Sarah if I could decorate my room with them. She told me it was fine with her. Those items were all just sitting around unused and collecting dust anyway. She was sure to let me know that I could not take them with me whenever I left my employment with them. She didn't need to tell me that, I would never have taken them anyway.

I found an old vase under the kitchen sink one day and asked if I could borrow it for my room. Oliver just waved his hand at me, the way he always did when I was annoying him, and said it was fine. I then took a few cuttings from the rose garden, hoping no one would care, and made myself a nice vase of roses for my room. I had to replenish it with new cuttings every week or so. No one seemed to notice. I always took the cuttings from the back of the bushes when no one was around. I had to be sneaky though. I didn't know if that was a fireable offense or not and I didn't want to find out the hard way. The gardener caught me one day and was really nice about it when I told him what I was doing. After that, I frequently found different flowers already cut and tied in a bunch waiting for me on the bench in the garden. He was a sweet man and I think he had a little crush on me.

I laid down on my bed to really think about what Violet had proposed. The whole thing was ridiculous, of course, but I have to admit, I was tempted. Never having to worry about money again would be the most fantastic thing to ever happen to me. But, could I actually seduce Adam, have his baby and give him or her away? That would be my own child after all. Could I live with giving my child away and never seeing him or her again? Did I trust Sarah to raise my baby right? And Violet. What kind of influence would she have? She had such an odd relationship with Adam and I didn't want that relationship to carry over to my child. I know that if I did give him or her up, I would have no say so in their upbringing. But, it all still made me nervous. I didn't want to turn my baby over to that family, unless I was pretty sure that it was the right thing to do. I thought Adam would be a good father. That part didn't bother me. It was Sarah and Violet that bothered me, and that gave me pause. Sarah wasn't a horrible person, but how would she feel about a child that her husband fathered with another woman? It made me nervous thinking about her hatred for me, and there definitely would be hatred when she found out I was pregnant with her husband's baby. Would that carry over to the baby? Could she love the baby as her own?

Could I do all of that for money? Did that make me a prostitute? Well, yes I guess it did. Having sex for money was the very definition of being a prostitute. What if I was being paid by someone other than the man I was sleeping with? Did that still count? If it wasn't technically prostitution, was it considered baby selling? If Violet gave me money to live on, just to help me out, would that be okay? I would just be giving the baby up for adoption technically, so it wasn't really baby selling, was it? I wasn't really sure of the answer and didn't know which was worse. One thing I did know for sure was that I was the one that would have to live with my decision and whichever label I imposed on myself.

I could probably continue questioning the whole thing and coming up with answers long enough to make it all seem right in my head. The money was terribly tempting. How could I turn it down? I would be set for life, never having to worry about anything ever again. Besides, I could have more children. Girls get pregnant on accident and give up their babies all the time. And they don't get paid for it. Maybe it would be a really smart thing for me to do. The difference was that I wouldn't be getting pregnant on accident and giving up my baby because I wasn't ready. I would be doing in on purpose. Even at 15 years old, that seemed like a really bad decision. And is that decision something I would have to explain to my adult child one day? He or she might want to know why things turned out the way they did. Ugh, so many things to consider. I started drifting off to sleep and decided I would worry about it the next day.

I spent a restless night tossing and turning, the decision weighing heavily on my mind. I got up early the next morning and knew what I would do. I didn't want to put off telling Violet what my decision was, so I went looking for her. It was time for her to know. After a while searching, she usually wasn't that hard to find, I found her in the formal dining room, sipping a cup of hot tea. She looked up from her newspaper as I walked in. She was wearing a bright yellow pantsuit. Believe me when I tell you, yellow was not her color.

"Abigail, dear, please come sit down."

So weird. She was never that nice to me. I guess she felt she needed to be nice to get me to agree to her crazy plan. She put her newspaper on the table as I sat down.

"How did you sleep?" she asked me.

"Um, not that great really," I told her honestly.

"I'm sorry to hear that. Was it due to our conversation from yesterday?" She seemed sincere in asking that question. She must have started in early drinking her special tea.

"Yes. Look, I have to tell you something. There is no way I can do what you asked. The money would be great, but it's just nuts. I would feel like a prostitute. I just can't do that."

"I see." That was all she said.

I waited for her to say something else. She didn't, so I figured the conversation was over and I got up to leave.

"Abigail, we are not finished." That stopped me in my tracks and I turned back toward her. I noticed her yellow pantsuit was almost glowing as the rays of the sun streamed through the picture window and seemed to seek her out.

I promptly sat down. I instinctively knew I was not going to like what was coming.

"What are your plans now?" She asked me.

I was genuinely confused. "I don't know what you mean." I responded. "Plans for what?"

"I think you do know exactly what I mean." She paused. "I made you an offer you really shouldn't refuse. You are young, no career goals, no prospects for a husband. So, I will ask you again. What are your plans?" She was obviously irritated with me and the tone of her voice sounded like she was challenging me. She held all the cards and she knew it.

I sat there in silence while I thought over what she had just said. Was she threatening me? It kind of sounded like it. Did she have some valid points? Probably. But I had my whole life ahead of me. I was only 15 years old. I still had plenty of time for all of those things to happen. I didn't need to trick some man into knocking me up so I could provide her an heir. I was starting to get more irritated the longer I thought about all she had just said to me.

"Look, you are right, I am still young and don't

really have a life plan mapped out yet. I currently have a job and a place to live, so I'm not desperate like I used to be. And as far as career goals, I want to be a chef someday. However, I still have lots of time to figure that all out. Besides, why in the world do I need a husband right now?" I knew I better tread carefully. I still needed this job and a place to live and didn't want to mess all of that up by blowing up at the rich old lady that owned the ranch. She terrified me.

Before she had a chance to respond, Adam walked in. I was saved again from Violet and her demands. I used that as an excuse to get out of there as fast as I could. I couldn't even look Adam in the eyes. I knew he was staring after me as I ran out of the room.

I avoided Violet as best I could after that, making sure we were never left in a room alone together. Believe me, it was not easy. Even in that enormous house, we ran into each other frequently. I usually just made some excuse about needing to make dinner or that I was heading to town for supplies, or something like that. It seemed to irritate her, because I'm sure she wanted to continue trying to convince me to go along with her insane plan. She even summoned me a couple of times, but I always found a way to get out of going to see her. Once I even pretended to sprain my ankle and had Sarah look at it. She said it seemed fine, but I limped around for a couple of days anyway, for emphasis. I don't know how convincing I was, but I didn't have to see Violet alone and I hadn't been fired yet. I just didn't know how long I could keep it up. Sooner or later I was going to have to talk to her again.

CHAPTER 10

Finally, I just couldn't stand trying to avoid Violet any longer and needed to get away for a while. I found John and convinced him to drive me into town for a shopping trip. He glared at me with those dark, scary eyes of his. Even though he drove me into town occasionally, we were definitely not friends. I was something he just tolerated.

John dropped me off at the local coffee house and said he would pick me up in a couple of hours. That was fine with me. I wanted to just get away for a while. I could walk around and do some window shopping if I got bored.

I found a table in the back corner of the coffee shop, near the bookshelves. I just loved the place with all of the paperbacks lining the walls that were free for the taking. Most people came in with a book and swapped them out when they were done. It was all on the honor system, and seemed to work pretty well, because the shelves were always packed with books. One of the employees came over and took my order. He was cute, maybe 18 years old, and really nice. I had seen him before, but never talked to him. While waiting for my coffee, I took one of the paperbacks off of the shelf, without even reading the description and just started reading it. After a few minutes I realized that I had read the same page three times and had no idea what I just read. Obviously I had other things on my mind and I couldn't concentrate on anything else. I was getting nowhere, so I put the book down and noticed my coffee was sitting there in front of me. When had it arrived? I didn't remember the waiter even coming back to the table. I guess I was really in my own head that afternoon.

All I could do was sulk about my issue with Violet. I knew I could not avoid her forever. Sooner or later she would corner me somewhere and I was scared of her. I knew that one word from her and I was out of a job and a place to live, all in an instant. I had saved up some money, but it wouldn't last that long. That would scare anyone in my situation.

"Are you okay?" I heard someone ask me and I looked up, a bit startled. It was my waiter.

"Oh, yes. Sorry, I didn't hear you walk up."

"No problem. You seem really upset and I wanted to check on you." He was very sweet.

He handed me a few napkins and that's when I noticed that there were tears streaming down my face.

"Oh my gosh, I'm so embarrassed," I said, wiping my face. "I guess I'm just having a bad day."

"It's okay. It happens to all of us. Would you like some company?" He didn't wait for me to answer and just sat down in the chair across from me.

"Um, I guess." He didn't seem to notice my apprehension with having a total stranger just invite himself to sit down with me.

"My name is Huck. What's yours?"

"It's Abbey. Nice to meet you." I wiped the tears from my face as I spoke to him.

He actually was very cute. He was around six feet

tall, had skin the color of warm mocha, short dark hair and greenish eyes that had a natural look of kindness to them. The dark skin and green eyes were an unusual, but very attractive combination. I bet he had no trouble at all with the ladies.

"Is your name really Huck?" I asked him.

There was definitely a strange look on my face. The name had to be made up. No one named their kid Huck anymore. Did anyone ever name their kid Huck?

He saw the look on my face and just smiled. "Yes, it really is my name. It's short for Huckleberry."

With that, my sadness was suddenly gone and I burst out laughing. I couldn't help it. It struck me as so funny that I doubled over in my chair and wrapped my arms around my waist while I laughed for at least a full minute. He just sat there patiently waiting for me to stop.

I finally looked up and noticed him watching me. "Oh my god, I'm so sorry. I really didn't mean to laugh at you." I was sincere in my apology, knowing that I had been incredibly rude, but I was still giggling just a bit.

"Are you done now?" he asked. He didn't seem upset at me at all and was very calm about the whole thing.

"Yes, again I'm sorry." I was finally serious and had stopped laughing. This time I picked up the napkins and wiped the laughter tears from my face, instead of the sad tears. There really was a difference.

"It's okay. Believe me, you are not the first, and won't be the last person to laugh at my name. It's an old family name and I kinda like it."

I liked him immediately.

"Well Huckleberry, why did you sit down anyway?"

"You seemed so unhappy, I felt it was my duty to cheer you up. I think I accomplished that." He sat back in his chair smiling, with a look of satisfaction on his face.

I smiled back. "Yes you did." I told him.

We sat there for hours chatting. It felt so natural talking to him. I didn't know this guy at all really, but everything just came pouring out. By the time I left, he knew pretty much my whole life story. I just knew I would never hear from him again. I probably sounded like a complete whacko.

However, I'm happy to say that I was completely wrong. After that day, we were almost inseparable. Huck became my best friend. I don't know how I would have survived my crappy life without him. He told me about his family and that his father was black and his mother was white and she had the same green eyes he had. He said they had been together forever and he loved them dearly.

It made me think about my own parents. I knew they loved me, and I knew that my problems with them were all of my own making. I even called them once from a pay phone when I was in town. When my mother answered, I lost my nerve and hung up on her. I don't know what was wrong with me. I was certain that if I asked, they would take me back in a heartbeat. But, I was humiliated at my behavior toward them, and everyone else. I just couldn't face them, and I couldn't face going back to school. Teenagers were the harshest of critics.

****

Violet continued to harass me, that's the only word that truly describes how it felt. She was not giving up, no matter how hard I tried to convince her that her idea was stupid and would never work. I didn't use those exact words, but you get the point. Finally one day I had had enough and I stopped her in the hallway to have a chat with her. I looked around carefully to make sure there were no prying ears nearby.

"Mrs. Tyler, can I talk to you?"

She stopped suddenly, shuffling back a step or two, obviously surprised that I initiated conversation with her, after she tried so often with me.

"Yes, but I'm not sure you and I have anything to talk about," was her curt response to me. "In fact, I have spoken with Adam about finding a replacement for you."

Oh my god, what have I done now? I would not survive without this job. I felt my throat closing up as I gasped for breath.

"Please, Mrs. Tyler, don't do that. I have nowhere to go," I choked out. Then I started crying, against my better judgment. I knew that I would have no leverage whatsoever if I broke down with her watching.

"That is not my problem. You should have thought of that before you rejected my generous offer."

She continued her walk down the long hallway. I

followed closely on her heels.

"Generous offer? Are you kidding me? You tried to pay me to seduce your son and have his baby!" I started yelling.

She stopped suddenly and started looking around. "You need to shut up right now," she whispered. "If anyone hears you, we are going to have really big problems."

She grabbed my right arm and dragged me into the nearest room, which happened to be the ballroom. She seemed surprised that the ballroom was where we ended up. She looked around and kind of rolled her eyes. "This will have to do, I guess," she told me.

"Look," I told her, yanking my arm away from her, "if you fire me, I will tell Adam what you wanted me to do."

I said it a little bit more quietly than I had intended. I meant to forcefully proclaim that I wasn't afraid of her threats, and had some threats of my own. But, it came out a bit shaky and scared sounding. Way to stand up for yourself, Abbey.

She hesitated for just a moment, trying to determine if I was bluffing or not. Then she stuck her nose up in the air and spoke kind of flippantly to me.

"I don't think you will tell Adam. Even though he hired you, don't you dare forget that this is my house. I own every thing and every one in it. That includes you. If you breathe a word of this to him, or to anyone for that matter, you will be out of this house so fast, you won't have time to come up with anymore threats. Do..I..make..myself..clear?" She said that last part slowly and methodically. I have to admit that she scared me.

"Y..yes," I stammered.

She glared at me one more time and turned on her heels and left me standing there staring after her. Violet Tyler was certainly a woman that was not to be messed with. I couldn't let her go, it would be the end of my life as I knew it. I would not survive on the streets again and was desperate to stay there. So, against my better judgment, I called after her.

"Mrs. Tyler, please wait," I said, as she was walking out the door.

She stopped suddenly and slowly turned to look at me. She didn't say a word.

"I'll do it." I couldn't believe the words were coming out of my mouth.

She just smiled and said, "then get on with with it," and walked out the door.

At that moment, I hated that woman with every bit of my soul.

CHAPTER 11

Adam and Sarah could not have been more different. Adam was kind, friendly and outgoing. He was definitely the boss and could be stern, true, but I found him to be endearing. Sarah, on the the other hand, was rude and standoffish. She wanted nothing to do with the employees, unless it was demeaning us. I think it was against her nature to be nice to the help. I'm not actually sure it was limited to the help. She didn't seem to ever be very nice to Adam either.

I spent the next couple of days trying to figure out how I was going to make this whole thing with Adam happen. I mean, I barely knew him. He was just my boss. My married boss. That was the toughest part. Seducing a married man to get pregnant on purpose had to be one of the lowest things ever. Besides, I had never actually seduced anyone before. I wasn't a virgin, having slept with a couple of guys when I was doing a lot of drugs with Josie. I was a bit ashamed about that, but what was done, was done. Actually making the decision to openly seduce someone was completely different, and I didn't have the slightest idea how to go about it. I still didn't know if I had it in me. Maybe I could stall for a while and wouldn't have to go through with it. Wishful thinking, I'm sure.

One afternoon, before dinner preparations started, I walked to the stables to get away from the kitchen for a bit. I just needed time to be alone and think, without Oliver and his non-stop chatter. It really did grate on the nerves after a while. Even the gossip that I used to enjoy was just getting old and I wished that he would stop. That wasn't going to happen though, so I got really good at tuning him out. Funny that he never noticed.

When I walked in to the stables, there was a strong odor of horses, hay, and old leather. I really liked it, and it was my favorite place to hang out. The horses were great listeners and did not judge me.

I think growing up on a ranch like Adam had done would have been just heavenly, and I fantasized about what my life would have been like being surrounded by all the horses and learning about raising and training them. I would have had many friends and we all would have run wild on the ranch. I smiled at that thought.

Whenever I went to the stables I always brought a few carrots and apples to give to the horses. I found the horses to be beautiful, highly intelligent creatures. After only a few days of showing up with their treats, I think they expected me to come. Whenever I walked into the stables, some of them would start dancing around in their stalls, in anticipation of their treats. Not all of them did it. Some of them pretty much ignored my presence and acted like I didn't exist. They took the fruit from me, but seemed to do it reluctantly. I told myself that those must be Sarah's horses, laughing out loud.

"What's so funny?"

I jumped when I heard the voice behind me. Spinning around, I found Adam leaning on a wall about twenty feet away from me. I wondered how long he had been there watching me. It made me uneasy.

"Um, nothing really. I'm just enjoying the horses. They seem to really like the apples."

"We should go riding sometime," he suggested, as he walked toward me.

"Oh, I couldn't do that. I've never ridden a horse before."

He seemed to be even better looking today, wearing jeans, a flannel shirt and cowboy boots. Usually he was a lot more formal. He didn't really wear suits much, but he did wear dressier clothes. I don't remember ever seeing him dressed like a cowboy. It suited him. I then turned back to give a carrot to Trixie, a beautiful chestnut thoroughbred. Rumor had it that she was worth a ton of money. That didn't matter to me. I just thought she was the sweetest thing ever.

"I could teach you." He smiled as he stepped right in front of me.

God, he was good looking. I suddenly felt my face get hot and I knew it was flushed. I turned back toward the horse again, hoping that he didn't notice me blushing.

"I don't know. These are really important horses and I don't want to hurt them or anything." I sounded like an idiot in my mind.

He chuckled. "I doubt you could hurt them. They are intelligent and very capable animals. Besides, I would teach you on one of the working horses. Those are the ones that the ranch hands ride. They are very gentle and used to being ridden. You would be perfectly safe on one of them."

I thought about it for a moment. "Well, okay, sure. I'd love to learn to ride. Will your wife be coming with us?" Against my better judgment, I really hoped the answer was no.

"Don't you worry, I'll take care of everything. Meet me here tomorrow morning, 8 a.m. Sharp," he said as I watched him walk back toward the house. I noticed I didn't get an answer to my question.

"You better watch yourself with that one," I heard someone say.

I turned around to see a pretty, dark haired girl standing in one of the stalls. The first thing I thought was 'why was everyone sneaking up on me today?'

"Oh, I didn't see you there," I said to her.

She continued brushing the horse she was with. "I know. I really wasn't trying to eavesdrop, but I was in here when Adam walked up and I didn't want to interrupt. My name is Teresa, by the way."

She was very pretty, about thirty years old, was my guess. She had medium length, brunette hair, and large brown eyes. I had seen her before working around the ranch, but we had never officially met.

"I'm Abbey."

"I know. You are the cook, right? You are very good at it." She had a really nice smile.

"Technically I'm the cook's assistant. But, thanks. So, what do you mean that I need to watch myself with him?" I knew what she meant. It was just nice to talk with a female for a change. The only other ones around were Violet and Sarah, and they both ignored me as much as possible.

"Adam Tyler is good looking, and charming, but he's married. You don't want to mess with that. I just want you to be really careful. You are young and could get yourself in trouble around him." She seemed sincere in her warning.

"I know, you are right."

I felt a little ashamed even accepting his offer to teach me to ride, even though I hadn't done anything wrong. Yet. There was no way I could tell her about the plan Violet and I had.

After we chatted for a bit, I went back inside to get started on dinner preparations. I thought about Teresa while I worked. She seemed nice enough. We could be friends. It would be really nice to have a friend around there. Walter was the only one that I even liked on the ranch, but he wasn't really best friend material for a 15 year old girl.

The next morning I arrived at the stables a bit early, because I was nervous and wanted to calm my nerves some before Adam showed up. I didn't want to be late and make a bad impression. When I arrived, I found that Adam had beaten me there and two of the horses were already saddled up and ready to go.

"I could have helped you with that. Isn't it something I should learn anyway?" I asked him.

"No need. There's always someone around that can saddle your horse for you. Riding is the fun part. Let someone else get the horses ready."

"Okay." I was there to learn and figured that's what

the ranch hands got paid for.

The day was just glorious for riding. The sun was shining bright with just a few wispy clouds in the sky. It was just cool enough for a light sweater, definitely a perfect day. Adam was wearing jeans, a long sleeved t-shirt and boots again. I don't know why I was surprised. I think those were pretty standard riding clothes. It was just still strange to me, because before yesterday I had never seen him dressed like that. He was very handsome.

Adam showed me how to get up on the horse and I found it was a lot easier than it looked. He said I was a natural. It sounded a bit flirty to me, but I brushed it off as my imagination. We started off very slowly and rode for perhaps an hour before we arrived back at the ranch. He took it very easy with me. We didn't run the horses at all. I was much too scared for that. He said he would save that for another day. We talked mostly about the horses and life on the ranch, nothing personal at all. He was very nice to me.

When we got back, Adam handed the horses off to one of the ranch hands and we headed inside. I felt kind of bad that I got to spend the day riding and didn't have to do anything but hand the the horses off afterward to someone else to attend to. I had always been a hard worker and didn't like making someone else do what I felt was something I should have done. It didn't seem to bother Adam though. I couldn't blame him, that's how he was raised. Besides I did see him often working with the horses. It wasn't as if he just sat in his office all day and did nothing else. From what I could see he worked very hard at keeping the horse farm running smoothly.

When we walked into the house together, Adam told me that he enjoyed teaching me to ride and we should do it again soon. That's when I noticed Sarah standing there, just inside the door. She had been waiting for us, that was obvious. She gave me a death look without saying a word. There was no need for her to say anything, I knew what she was thinking. We hadn't done anything wrong, but I suddenly felt very guilty. I dropped my eyes quickly to the floor and scurried, that's the best word to describe it, to the kitchen to get to work. I then had to explain to Oliver why I was late. He didn't seem any happier than Sarah did. I wasn't making any friends that day.

CHAPTER 12

Two days later Adam asked me if I wanted another lesson.

I hesitated before answering him. "I don't know. Your wife seemed really upset when she saw the two of us together the other day."

"Oh, don't worry about her," he said, waving his hand in a flippant manner. "I explained that I was just teaching you how to ride, and she was fine."

I didn't really believe him. I saw the look on Sarah's face. But, if he said it was okay, how could I argue with him? I agreed to another lesson and we had a great time. Over the next few weeks I really started to like him. He was fun to be around and I got to be a pretty good rider. One day after we had been training for a little while, we sat down on the bank of the river for a break. It wasn't a very wide river, but it was just beautiful and kind of meandered along at a nice pace. A flock of white birds flew over and I was mesmerized as I watched them until they were out of sight.

"You don't like my wife much, do you?" he asked me out of the blue and it startled me back to reality.

There was a soft breeze from the river and it had blown a few strands of hair into my face. I reached up to brush them away as I thought about how I was going to answer that question. Was there any answer that wouldn't get me into trouble?

"Well..." was all I could muster at that moment. "I..."

"It's okay, you don't have to answer," he interrupted. "I know."

I just looked at him with a half smile, really not knowing how to respond. Regardless of how I felt about her, there was no way I was going to say anything negative about his wife. I wasn't that stupid.

"I know Sarah can be trying at times. But, she's not all bad."

"I'm sure she's not. I don't know her very well. I think she avoids me whenever she can," I told him honestly.

"We haven't been married all that long and I do love her in my own way. My parents pretty much made me marry her. It wasn't really an arranged marriage, I mean I did agree to it, which was after my parents strongly insisted that we marry. They knew her parents and well. You know how it goes."

"No, I really don't. My parents would never make me marry anyone I didn't want to marry." That was true.

"They didn't really make me." He started to sound a bit defensive, crossing his arms over his chest.

"Oh, I'm sorry. I didn't mean to upset you." I was afraid that I would make him mad. I desperately needed at least one ally in the Tyler family.

"I know. I just meant that our marriage certainly isn't something that fairy tales are made from, but it pretty much works for us. When Henry and Violet Tyler wanted something, it usually happened. I knew I couldn't fight it, so there really was no point. Besides, Sarah is a decent catch, even though I know that I will never be deeply, truly in love with her. We can make it work." He sounded like he was trying quite hard to convince himself, instead of me.

He was spilling his guts to me, which was crazy. I barely knew him and didn't even know what to say. The conversation was turning very personal and I felt like an outsider that was eavesdropping. I certainly didn't feel comfortable enough to make any comments about the state of his family. Therefore, I mostly kept my mouth shut. It was all very personal stuff he really shouldn't be telling one of his employees.

"Oh, I'm making you feel uncomfortable. I'm sorry," he told me.

Apparently he could see how reluctant I was to speak about the topic when it was not my place to do so.

"No, it's okay. I just have never been married and can't relate."

He smiled at me and stood up then, reaching out his hand to help me up. "Come on. We should be getting back."

The ride back to the ranch was pretty quiet. We chatted about the horses and other things. There was no more talk about his marriage at all. I was relieved.

****

The next day I was in the kitchen prepping for lunch and in walked Violet Tyler. Oliver and I looked at each other in shock. I remember Oliver telling me that in all the years he had been working there, Violet had never been in the kitchen. Even though she owned the house, he was pretty sure she had no idea where the kitchen was.

"Abigail, I would like to speak to you. Alone." She was looking directly at Oliver as she said this. He just put his knife down on the counter and walked out without saying a word.

I watched him as he left, then turned my attention to Violet.

"Abigail, I want an update on the Adam situation," she demanded.

Luckily she kept her voice low. I certainly didn't need Oliver overhearing anything. It would be all over the ranch before Violet left the kitchen.

"Um, well, there really is not much to tell," I said quietly.

"Why not? You have had weeks. Do you not know how to seduce someone?" Wow, right to the point.

"Not really, no." The admission embarrassed me. How lame that I didn't know how to make a man like me. Wasn't that something that all females knew how to do instinctively?

"Well figure it out. This is taking far too long. I expect some better news in a few days."

Apparently she was done with me, because she walked out without another word. I heard her speaking with Oliver in the hall and he walked in a minute later. He gave me a quizzical look, but I wasn't about to spill the beans about my 'arrangement' with Violet. I was absolutely ashamed that I had even agreed to it in the first place.

That afternoon Huck came by the house for a visit.

I had an hour or so until I had to get back to work, so we went for a walk around the ranch. We just talked and went to see the horses for a bit. Teresa was there. She and I had become friends over the last few weeks. I didn't dare tell her about Adam though. She had seen us together several times and made a comment here and there, but mostly stayed out of it. I did appreciate that.

I introduced Huck to Teresa and they hit it off immediately. They started chatting and completely forgot I was even standing there for several minutes. Finally, I tugged at Huck's sleeve and he tore himself away from her and continued his walk with me.

I think Teresa had a thing for him, because every time he came over after that, she always showed up. He didn't seem to mind because they were friends. It was starting to irritate me. I don't think he was interested in her though, as he had a crush on me. I know this because he asked me out a few times. I thought he was cute and funny and was a great guy, but I didn't think of him that way. He was my friend and that's all it would ever be. Besides, with everything that was in the works with Adam, I couldn't possibly get involved with anyone else. How in the world would something like that even work?

A few days later I ran into Adam as I was walking out of my room to go to work one afternoon.

"Oh, sorry," I said as I tried to walk around him.

"No wait, I was looking for you," he said, blocking my way.

"You were?" I looked up into his beautiful green

eyes.

"Yeah, I want to show you something. Come with me." He started walking toward the stairs.

"Wait, I can't. I'm late for work."

"Don't worry about that. Did you forget that I'm the boss? I'll tell Oliver it was my fault. Come on." He smiled and I followed.

I'm sure Oliver is going to love that, I thought as I followed him up to the second floor, and then up another flight of stairs to the third floor. It was eerily quiet. Rarely did anyone use the third floor. We continued walking to the end of the hallway to one of the bedrooms.

"Come in." He stood in the doorway, stepping aside so I could go in first.

I was a bit leery, but went on in anyway. This one was a bit different than the other rooms I had been in. It was beautifully decorated, as every room in the entire house was, but as we walked inside, Adam walked over and opened a closet door.

"What's in the closet that I need to see?" I asked him, wondering what in the world was going on. I was a bit suspicious.

He smiled that gorgeous smile of his. "It's not a closet, come on."

I walked over and was surprised to find that it was another bedroom. From outside, it just looked like a closet. So it was kind of a secret room, I guessed. At least it seemed that way to me. I walked in and it was really cozy. It was still a good sized room, but decorated in browns and reds. It was really different and felt very comfortable and cozy. It wasn't decorated like a hunting lodge, but kind of had that feel. Very down to earth. It made me just want to curl up under a blanket, in front of the fireplace. Yes, there was a fireplace in this 'secret room'. I walked around, just taking it all in. I loved everything about the room.

"Do you like this painting?" He asked, pointing to a large painting on the wall.

I looked at it with all of its bright colors and odd shapes, and loved it immediately. "It's beautiful. Did you paint it?"

He burst out laughing. "Hardly."

"What's so funny?" I was a bit embarrassed that he started laughing at me.

"That, my dear, is an original Picasso." He looked very pleased with himself with that announcement.

"Wait, what? No way." I looked at him for confirmation.

"Yes, it really is. Picasso himself gave it to my grandfather. They were friends many years ago when my grandfather lived in Spain." It was obvious that he was trying to impress me. It worked.

"Wow, that's just crazy. That thing must be worth a fortune."

"It is. There are very few people that even know it's here. None of the staff know it is a Picasso. We are afraid of it being stolen."

"I don't blame you. I would be worried about that too. So why are you telling me? Aren't you afraid I will take off with it?" It was an honest question.

"You? No, never. I trust you." He looked at me seriously and I knew he meant it.

"You are right. I am a lot of things, but not a thief," I told him.

Okay, I used to be a thief, but those days were over. I had vowed never to do that again. I was horribly ashamed of my past. Adam didn't know any of it and I could never tell him.

"I do love this painting though. It's really too bad that it is hidden away up here and not down in the library or ballroom for everyone to enjoy."

"Sarah refuses to let me hang it up downstairs. She doesn't even know where it is and thinks I just stuck it in storage somewhere. She hates it. She knows what it's worth, but Picasso is not her 'cup of tea'. She loves realism in her art."

"Even so," I replied, "I don't know how in the world she can not love this. Well, I guess you can't please everyone."

"We should go." He suddenly said. "We've been up here a while and people will start looking for us. I'll go have a talk with Oliver for you, so you don't get in trouble with him. I know he can be difficult."

"Thanks, that would be really nice. And thanks for showing me this. It's just amazing," I told him as we made our way back down to the kitchen.

CHAPTER 13

The next day, Adam found me out in the garden, reading. Apparently, there was nowhere on the ranch that I could hide from him. Or from anyone for that matter.

"I would like to talk to you about something." He started speaking without even waiting for me to finish the chapter I was on. I hated to stop reading when I was in the middle of a chapter.

He seemed impatient, so I went ahead and put my book down and looked up as he sat down next to me.

"I have a friend that owns a zoo not far from here. Would you like to go see it? That's not weird is it?" He seemed a bit hesitant.

"Why would a zoo be weird? I love zoos. Will there be a group of us going?" I was pretty sure I already knew the answer.

"Well, no. I meant just you and me." He paused for a moment to gauge the reaction on my face.

"Oh, I see. Well sure. When do you want to go?" I asked him.

He reached up and brushed some strands of hair from my face. It was a very gentle and loving gesture. For a minute I thought he was going to kiss me. It took only a couple more seconds to realize that that would never happen. Not here, sitting in the garden, where anyone could see us. I could feel that he was starting to fall for me, but he wasn't a stupid man. He would wait.

"How about tomorrow night, after they close? We

would have the whole place to ourselves."

I'm sure the look on my face was a bit fearful, but he just sat there and waited for my response. I knew that if this thing that Violet cooked up was ever going to happen, I actually needed to do something.

"Okay, sure," I replied.

We both knew this was a date. I knew he was married and what we were doing was so completely wrong. I knew this made me a terrible person, but I didn't see any way out of it. I did like Adam. He was very good looking and charming. Who wouldn't be attracted to that, and to everything he had to offer? However, there was Sarah. He belonged to her. I had no right to him and I knew it.

He smiled. "Great. Sarah's gone for a few days. She went to visit her sister, Jackie, and nephew, Jackson. But, people talk. So, why don't you meet me out by the road at 8 p.m.? Is that okay with you? I just don't want to give them anything else to gossip about, you know?"

I knew.

"Sure, that's fine," I relented.

****

The next night, I walked out to meet Adam by the road. It was dark, so I probably couldn't be spotted easily. Yes, I was going to meet a married man, my boss even, but I refused to skulk in the bushes. I decided that I wasn't going to worry about it and I walked straight down the middle of the long driveway toward the road. Even if someone came along and stopped to talk to me, they wouldn't know what I was up to. Unless they could read the guilt that was all over my face.

I could see headlights coming down the driveway behind me and I moved over to the left side to let the car go by. It slowed down as it came near me, and I could see that Adam was driving. He looked over at me, but kept going. Wow, really? I looked around and there was not a soul in sight. No one would have seen him pick me up in the dark, so far from the house.

"Would it have killed you to pull over and pick me up back there?" I chided him as I climbed into the passenger seat a few minutes later. He had actually come around and opened the door for me, which was very sweet. He was wearing slacks and a nice button down shirt. He looked very nice. I had dressed up too. I still didn't have anything fancy, but was making some money, and bought a cute dress and sandals.

"Sorry. I just figured it was better to get off the ranch before anyone saw us together." He seemed a little embarrassed.

I didn't respond.

We made small talk on our drive over to the zoo. It was obvious that we were both nervous. I had never been on a real date before. Yes, I had a couple of boyfriends in high school, but we just hung out. We never went on actual dates. So, this was all new to me.

When we arrived, I was really surprised at the sight of it all. I expected some worker to be waiting for us in front of a dark zoo to let us in. But, that wasn't the case. The front of the zoo had white lights strung everywhere. It was so beautiful. Magical even. Adam got out of the car, walked around to my side and opened my door for me. I just smiled at him. He then opened the back passenger door and reached in for something. I was surprised when he pulled out a picnic basket.

"I've prepared a nice meal for us," he explained when I asked him about the basket.

"*You* prepared it?" I asked him, with a silly smirk on my face. He laughed.

"Well, okay, you caught me. I didn't prepare it myself. My friend owns a restaurant in town and he had it made up for me. He doesn't ask questions."

"I see."

Had he done this before? Was I just another one in a long line of girlfriends? Maybe. No, probably not. Even though he was married and we were on a date, I doubted that Adam made a habit of cheating on his wife. On the other hand, I could be completely wrong. It's been known to happen.

"Can you carry this blanket?" he asked, handing it to me before I had a chance to answer.

He closed both car doors and led me over to the entrance of the zoo. He then pulled a key from his pocket and opened the front gate for me. It was mostly quiet, the animals had probably bedded down for the night, but I could hear a growl and a squawk off in the distance. It was a bit unnerving. I knew they were all locked up tight. But, knowing that we were the only two people there, with hundreds of dangerous, wild animals surrounding us, was a bit scary.

We walked slowly through the zoo for about ten

minutes, until we reached a nice grassy area near the aviary. He sat the picnic basket down and took the blanket that was draped over my arm from me, spreading it out on the grass. He then gestured for me to have a seat. I was very nervous when I sat down. He sat down next to me and started taking things from the basket. I was surprised by how much it held. It was quite a spread, consisting of delicious looking food from the French restaurant his friend owned. He poured both of us a glass of wine to start, and we ate dinner while enjoying the peacefulness of the zoo.

"This is really beautiful. I've never been in a zoo alone, in the dark before," I told him.

"You aren't alone."

"You know what I mean. This is just really nice. Thank you for bringing me here."

"You don't have to thank me. It's my pleasure. I've been really looking forward to us being alone together for a change. Away from the ranch, I mean," He told me.

"Yeah, me too." I replied.

"I want to tell you something," he said, as we were finishing up our meal. "I think I'm falling in love with you." He looked at me for a response, his eyes hopeful.

I took a deep breath. "I think I'm falling in love with you too," I responded. It was the truth. We had spent a lot of time together over the last several weeks. I knew it was wrong, but I loved him. I couldn't help myself.

That's when he leaned over and kissed me for the first time. It was a gentle, loving kiss. He had the softest lips. He made me feel like I had never been kissed before and I just melted into him. We made love right there, while listening to the animals nearby. I kind of felt like we were being watched. Actually, we probably *were* being watched.

Afterward, common sense hit me upside the head. "What are we doing?" I said a bit too loudly, pushing him away.

"You know what we are doing," he replied, reaching for me. "You knew what you were getting yourself into when you agreed to come here with me."

"You are married. We can't do this."

"I know, you're right. But, I love you," he responded, taking me into his arms again. Like that made it all okay. But, it wasn't okay.

"I love you too, but that's not the point. You know we shouldn't be here." I pushed him away again.

"I want to keep seeing you," he told me.

"What about Sarah? What if she finds out?" I was definitely worried about that.

"How is she going to find out? I'm not going to tell her, are you?"

"Of course not."

This made me think. Did I really want to be with a man that would cheat on his wife, and not be sorry about it? What if we got married someday? Would he do the same thing to me? Married to Adam. I can't believe I was even thinking about that. He would never divorce Sarah. Would he? No, Violet would never allow that.

****

The next morning, right after we were finished serving and cleaning up after breakfast, I walked into town to see Huck. He smiled when he saw me walk in and sit down at my usual table. He walked over with a coffee and muffin and sat them down in front of me. Then he sat down.

"Thanks."

"Sure. Are you okay? You look a bit depressed," he told me.

I'm sure he was right. I was up most of the night thinking about Adam and how in the world I was going to deal with all of it. I had dragged myself to work that morning and got through it, barely. Oliver yelled at me a couple of times when he noticed I was dragging along. He was right, of course. As soon as I was finished, I told Oliver that I would be back in a couple of hours, and I left for town.

"Well, I did something I shouldn't have."

"Really? What?" He asked me, while reaching over and pinching off a piece of my blueberry muffin and taking a bite.

"I slept with Adam last night." I said it very quietly and looked down at my plate in shame.

"You what?!" he almost yelled. I looked around to see if anyone had heard him. A couple people looked over curiously, but went back to their conversations when I gave them a look.

I didn't even respond to that. I was so ashamed.

"I can't freaking believe you did that. What in the

world were you thinking!"

"Please stop yelling. You're embarrassing me," I whispered to him.

"Sorry, okay." He calmed down then, looking around. No one seemed to be paying any attention to us. "Why did you do that?" He was much quieter.

"Because I love him." It was a stupid answer. Love did not justify my actions and I knew it.

"Are you being serious with me right now?" He didn't believe me.

"Yes I am. I can't help how I feel."

"What about his wife? Did you forget all about her?" He was obviously angry with me.

"No, I didn't forget about Sarah. But, we love each other." I heard myself, and still couldn't believe I was saying those words.

"You need to break it off with him," he told me matter-of-factly.

"No, I can't do that." An argument was coming. I could feel it in the air.

"Yes you can. If you don't, then you are going to have big problems. His wife will find out, she will fire you and maybe divorce Adam. Do you want to be responsible for all of that and be out on the streets again?"

He had some really valid points.

"None of that is going to happen. Just leave me alone!" I yelled. This time everyone in the cafe turned to look at us. "Mind your own damn business!" I yelled at them as I stormed out.

Huck didn't follow me and I was just fine with that. If he couldn't understand how much I loved Adam, then that was his problem.

****

A few days later Huck called me at the house. "I'm sorry," he told me. "I'm just worried about you." He seemed sincere.

"I know. I'll be careful, I promise."

"You'll be careful about what?" I spun around to see Violet standing in the doorway of the library, where I was talking on the phone.

"I've gotta go," I told Huck and hung up the phone.

"Nothing," I said to Violet. "Look, I need to talk to you about something."

She just stood there waiting for me to explain.

"I can't do this. I can't get pregnant on purpose."

"I see. Then what was the other night?" She asked me.

My face lit up with surprise. What did she know about that? She couldn't possibly know. Was she bluffing? That seemed like an odd bluff, if she had no idea at all that we had started seeing each other.

"I see by the surprise on your face that you have no idea what I know."

"I don't know what you are talking about," I tried to deflect. I didn't think it was going to work.

"Yes you do. I know about your date with Adam at the zoo."

I was in shock. She did know. How was that possible? I didn't even respond. What could I say?

"You underestimate me, Abigail. I know a lot of people in town and they keep me informed of anything having to do with my family." She seemed satisfied with herself and smirked at me.

"Oh." That was all I could force out of my mouth.

"So, it seems that you decided to take me up on my offer after all?"

"Yes...I mean no," I blurted out.

"Which is it? Yes or no?" She seemed to be much more patient than usual.

"It's no. I don't want to do this."

"It looks to me like you already did."

Wow, she really did know what was going on. Was someone watching us in the zoo? All of us sudden I felt really dirty.

"Well...I know. I don't want to lie to Adam though. I think I love him." I don't know why I told her that. It wasn't going to help my case.

"Is that right?" She was so smug.

"Yes, that's right. I love him and I can't lie to him. He loves me too. He told me so. I want to keep seeing him, but I won't get pregnant. I wouldn't do that to him." Even as I was saying them, I couldn't believe the words that were coming out of my mouth.

"We will see about that." She then turned around and walked out the door.

There was no telling what that woman would do, and I was suddenly very afraid of Violet Tyler.

CHAPTER 14

Adam and I continued to see each other. We met when we could and I don't think anyone caught on. At least no one said anything to either one of us about it, not that I expected anyone too. Unless it was Violet or Sarah, I was pretty sure no one would have the nerve to bring it up in conversation. How would that go anyway? Something like: 'I heard you and Adam are having a wild fling behind his wife's back.' No, I don't think that would happen.

The weird thing was that Violet was strangely quiet about the whole thing. She obviously knew, but didn't mention it again. Oh, she was still hateful to me, that wasn't going to change. But, she didn't bring up Adam and me again. It almost would have been better if she had bugged me about it. At least then I would know where she stood. The silent treatment regarding Adam was unnerving. Unfortunately, I didn't have anyone I could even talk to about it, and I wanted that desperately. It was hard keeping everything all bottled up inside. Huck hated the idea of Adam and me together, so that was out of the question. He just didn't understand. I didn't feel close enough to have that conversation with Teresa about her boss. That would just be weird. I thought about calling Josie, my friend from high school, but thought better of it. Nothing good could come from me calling her. She was my worst influence. I just didn't need that, or her, in any part of my life again. And there was no one else. So, I just kept it all to myself, as sad as that was.

One day Adam found me and asked me if I would like to go away for a weekend.

"Exactly how is that going to work?" I asked him in disbelief that he would even suggest it.

Did he completely forget that he had a wife and we all lived in the same house? People would notice us both being gone at the same time. I thought that Sarah might be suspicious of us, even though she couldn't know anything for sure. We were very discreet. At least I think we were. So, assuming that she didn't know anything for sure, it sounded like a bad idea for both of us to be away at the exact same time.

"I go on a lot of business trips, as you know. So that part will seem completely normal. Then I'll just tell Sarah and Oliver that you asked me for the weekend off. I'll say you want to go visit your parents or something. You never take time off. They can't really argue with me about it."

"Won't that look suspicious?" Sarah and Oliver were not stupid people.

"No. I'll tell them today about you. Then after you go into town and wait for me on Friday, I'll tell Sarah I got called to another ranch for a meeting and will be back on Monday. It happens all the time. No one will be the wiser." He seemed so confident.

It seemed like he had it all worked out. "Well, okay. If you think it will work, then I'm in."

Adam smiled. "It will. Leave everything to me."
***

The next weekend we left without a hitch. No one

seemed to suspect, or even care, for that matter. I had John drive me into town, telling him that a friend was picking me up for the weekend. It wasn't a lie. He dropped me off at the library, where I waited for Adam. I didn't want to go to the coffee house because I didn't want Huck to see Adam and me together. Not that it was any of his business, but I just didn't need the grief. So, I hid out in the library until Adam arrived a little while later.

    We had a wonderful time. We drove to the airport and flew all the way to California. I had never been on an airplane before and I loved it. I just didn't get people who were afraid of flying. What was the big deal? I had never been to California before and it was wonderful. We saw a few of the sights, but honestly, we didn't spend a lot of time outside our room and we loved every minute of it. We stayed at a place called The Wildflower Inn, and it was just perfect. It was right on the beach, with a cute little outdoor cafe that had a wonderful view of the water. The teenagers that worked there were running around in beach wear and flip flops. It looked like the funnest job ever. If it weren't for Adam, I might have stayed and worked there, right at the beach.

    It was so nice to not have to sneak around. At home, we were always afraid of being caught and had to be really careful. In California, I didn't know a soul and we could do what we wanted. I didn't expect to get to go on trips like that often, or maybe ever again, so we just enjoyed ourselves with the little time we had. Adam spoiled me, buying me expensive meals and sight seeing trips and even some cute souvenirs. I figured I was going to have to hide them when I got back to the ranch. No one would ever believe that I just flew out to California for the weekend with a friend. It would look really suspicious to show up with souvenirs from there. I would have be careful.

****

When we arrived home, separately of course, we were surprised at what we found. Violet was in the middle of planning a huge party in the ballroom. Even though I would have to work during the party, I was as excited as everyone else. According to Oliver it had been a really long time since such a huge event had taken place there, and I had never witnessed one.

I got thrown right into the middle of all the planning and it was so much fun. I asked Violet what the occasion was and she said it was just because she wanted to. There was no need to have another reason. Life was much too short to wait around for parties to happen. I couldn't agree more.

The day of the party came way too fast. We spent the entire day putting everything together in the ballroom. So much to do, but it all got done. Then everyone started arriving. Hundreds of people showed up, even some of the people that worked on the ranch. Not the house staff or the ranch hands, but people with a little more prestige, such as Teresa. As the head horse trainer, she was invited. So were a few of the people that helped Adam manage the ranch. I knew most of them, but since I wasn't a guest, I wasn't allowed to mingle with them. Teresa brought Huck as her guest.

That was a little weird because he was invited and I wasn't. Oh well, I guess I had my place. I had made my peace with it.

I heard many of the guests talking about Violet and her wonderful parties. They missed coming to them. I had such a nice time just hanging out. It was a great party, one like I had never been to before. The parties I went to back home were so completely different. Everyone that went to those were there just to get high and drunk. At this party, they were there to see old friends and talk and laugh. There was still a lot of alcohol being consumed, but it was a different vibe. They weren't all there for the sole purpose of getting drunk. I could get used to this kind of party.

Even though I was working, and not an invited guest, I really didn't have a lot to do. A lot of people were hired to take care of the food, music, drinks, and all that during the party. My job of helping to plan and set up was pretty much done. So, I stood there just watching people mostly, and helping out here and there when needed.

As I was standing by the buffet, deep in thought, someone walked up beside me, which brought me back into the moment. I noticed immediately how cute he was and smiled to myself. He was probably 17 or 18 years old and just started talking to me out of nowhere. He told me that his name was Ben and that he was a bit bored, because most of the people at the party were well over 30, and many closer to Violet's age. It was her party after all. Not many were teenagers, so I guess that's why he sought me out. He was really friendly and we hit it off. He was easy to talk to and we started flirting a bit. It was all just harmless fun.

At one point during our conversation I looked over and noticed Adam watching us intently, with a scowl on his face. It was a little unnerving.

"Are you okay?" Ben asked me. I guess I wasn't hiding my uneasiness very well.

"What?..Oh, yes, I'm fine." Stuttering a bit, I tore my eyes away from Adam and tried to concentrate on Ben.

"Well, you seem upset all of a sudden."

"No. No, I'm fine. Sorry, I just lost my concentration for a minute." I tried to sound calm.

Without even talking to Adam, I could see by his expression that he was very unhappy watching me flirt with Ben. I tried my best to ignore him, but it wasn't working. I kept looking over at him, without even meaning to.

"What do you keep looking at?" Ben asked me, while looking in the direction my eyes were pointed in.

I quickly turned to look at him. "Nothing. Don't worry about it. I just thought I saw someone I knew. So, what were we talking about?"

Just then, I felt someone grab my arm and yank me away from my conversation. I looked up to see that it was Adam. I was shocked and I gave him an incredulous stare. What in the world could he have possibly been thinking, grabbing me away from Ben like that, in front of everyone? He pulled me out the staff's entrance door, into the hallway that led to the kitchen. I didn't even have to look behind me to know that there were lots of curious eyes watching us. I wondered what in the world Ben must have been thinking at that moment. He did nothing to stop Adam though. What could he possibly do anyway? Adam was the heir to the ranch. I doubt anyone would have challenged him. Adam knew that too.

"What the hell are you doing?" Adam hissed at me once the door to the ballroom was closed and he had scanned the hallway for prying ears.

I yanked my arm away from him. "What are you talking about?"

"That guy. Who is that?" His green eyes flared with anger.

"I don't know. Ben. I just met him. He came with his parents."

"Well I don't like it."

Just then one of the catering staff pushed past us with a tray of food. Adam opened the door for her. We could hear the music and conversations waft in. Obviously, there wasn't a crowd standing there with their ears all glued to the door. It seemed that no one cared where we went. There was a lot of free flowing booze. Maybe no one would even remember him manhandling me out the door.

"I don't really care if you like it. We were just talking. Do I not have the right to have a conversation with someone now? What am I, your property?" I knew I was being defiant, and was probably going to make matters worse, but at that moment I didn't care. He had a wife and I was not throwing a temper tantrum in the middle of a huge party whenever he talked to her.

Snapping at Adam seemed to calm him down a bit. That wasn't the reaction I expected at all. Just the opposite actually.

"Of course you are not my property. I just want you all to myself. I hate to admit it, but it really bothers me when you talk to other guys." He seemed sincere and was at least being honest.

"Yeah, I can tell. Adam, you have nothing to worry about. You are the one I'm with. The one I want. Not him. I was just trying to pass the time. Ben was bored and wanted someone to talk to. That's it. I seriously doubt I'll ever see him again after tonight."

"I certainly hope not."

"I.." Just as I started to protest, we were interrupted when Sarah came walking through the door from the ballroom, looking for Adam.

She took one look at the both of us and frowned. "What's going on in here? I was looking for you and your mother said she saw the two of you headed this way. She said you looked angry." She was speaking directly to Adam.

"Nothing's going on," Adam replied. "I just needed to talk to Abbey about the food. Everything's fine. Let's go."

With that, he put out his elbow for her to take and they walked back into the ballroom together. He never even looked back at me. He had the nerve to yell at me for just talking to another man, while he was still married and hiding me from everyone. I knew why, but

I still didn't like it.

I took a couple of minutes to take some deep breaths and calm down before I returned to the party. Thanks to Adam, I just wanted to go to my room and forget about everything for a while. I heard a voice call after me as I was walking through the party toward the exit.

"Abbey!" It was Huck.

I stopped to see what he wanted.

"Are you okay?" he asked me.

"What do you mean?"

"I saw Adam drag you out of the ballroom. We all saw him do it. You were the talk of the party after that." Huck told me.

"Oh great, just what I need."

"What happened?" It didn't seem that he was going to let it go.

"Nothing. He just wanted to talk to me about the food." I hoped Adam's story to Sarah would work on Huck too.

"I don't believe you. I watched him force you out of the room. He looked really mad." Huck did appear to be genuinely concerned about me.

"No. Don't be so dramatic. It was nothing. Look, I'm not feeling very well, so I'm going to my room to lay down. Please just go back to the party. I'm sure Teresa doesn't appreciate being left all alone so you can come over and talk to me." With that I walked out.

CHAPTER 15

During the next few months, Huck and I became even closer friends and I loved him dearly. My life would not be the same without him. He had been dating Teresa, the ranch's horse trainer, for a little while. Even though there was about a ten year age difference, they seemed like a great fit. I knew they were happy together. Teresa and I became closer friends too. We all hung out a lot, mostly at the coffee house. It was really nice having people around that cared for me. I had missed that.

We had many deep conversations about our families and our lives. Huck knew more about me than anyone else on the planet, and I just adored him. He spoke often about his little sister, Madison. She died a while back from cancer. It was obvious that it was still very painful for him. Because she was several years younger than him, there was no sibling rivalry between the two of them. She was the love of his life by the way he talked about her. He would have done anything for her. But, no matter what, he couldn't save her. I could tell that tore him apart. As much as he talked about Madison, I felt like I knew her, even though she died long before Huck and I ever met. It was comforting knowing that he could love someone so deeply. I knew we would always be best friends. I wasn't as close with Teresa, but I still liked her very much.

One day, Huck and I had lunch while Teresa was at work. I had the day off and we were just walking around town window shopping. The afternoon was a bit cool and breezy. When it started raining, we ducked into the library. I had only been there once, briefly, when waiting for Adam to show up for our trip. But that time I didn't spend any time exploring the library. I just waited at a table for Adam. This time I paid more attention. It was the cutest, most charming library I had ever seen. It even had a small coffee shop in it. Well, more like a coffee counter with a couple of tables nearby. We both ordered a hot coffee to warm us up and sat down at one of the tables to wait out the storm.

We made small talk for a few minutes, but Huck seemed to have something else on his mind. Something that he wasn't talking about. He seemed distant and distracted.

"What is it?" I asked him.

"What do you mean?" He looked confused.

"You have something on your mind. Spill," I told him with a smile.

"Oh. Well, okay. Um, you know that I've been seeing Teresa for a little while now, right?" It wasn't really a question. He knew that I was well aware of their relationship. We had all hung out many times.

"Yeah, so?"

"Well, I don't think I want to see her anymore."

"What? Why?" I was really surprised. I thought they were happy together and I really liked Teresa. I didn't want to see them split up.

"Um, well, there's someone else. I think I'm in love with someone else." He couldn't look me in the eyes.

"Really? Who?" The conversation was finally starting to get interesting.

"I don't know. Never mind." He looked out the window. "The rain is starting to let up. We should go."

He started to get up out of his chair and I reached across the table and grabbed his arm. "Whoa, wait a minute partner. You are not getting away that easy," I said as I pulled him gently back into his chair. "I am your best friend and you need to tell me who it is, right now, before I hurt you." I gave him my best cheesy smile. He couldn't help but smile back.

"No, I can't. I don't think you are going to like it." He stared into his coffee.

"Why not? I mean Teresa is nice, but if she isn't the one for you, you need to be with the one you love. Is it a guy? It is, isn't it? Is that what all the secrecy is about?" I knew he wasn't gay. It was just fun teasing him.

"Okay, now I'm leaving." He pretended to be angry and started rising from his chair. He wasn't mad. He was teasing back.

"Okay, okay. I'm sorry. I was just kidding. But really, who is she?" I really wanted to know. He sat back down again.

"Well, all right. I guess I started this whole thing, no getting out of it now. It's you, okay? You are the one I want to be with."

Dead silence. That was not what I was expecting at all and I had no idea how to respond. I knew he had a crush on me, but I thought that was over when he started getting serious with Teresa. I guess I was wrong.

"Oh," was the only sound I could make. I think I was in shock.

"It's okay, you don't have to say anything. I just thought you should know." He seemed embarrassed by his proclamation of love. I could tell he wanted to take it all back. Too late for that. I couldn't unhear it.

"Look, Huck, you know that I'm in love with Adam. I haven't made it a secret. Not with you anyway." I felt really bad, all of a sudden.

"I know. He's terrible for you though. That can never go anywhere. He's married and he is the heir to a fortune. His mother would never, ever allow him to divorce Sarah and marry you. I'm sorry, but that's the truth."

He wasn't wrong. Even still, I had to defend myself.

"No, you're wrong. I have no idea how, but we are in love and will figure it all out. I know he wants to be with me, not his wife. I don't know what we are going to do about Sarah, but Violet won't live forever." It wasn't a threat, but almost sounded like one.

I continued. "You know I love you. You are my best friend. But, it's not the same thing that I feel for Adam." I put my hand over his on the table in a comforting gesture. He pulled his hand back away from me. I understood. "I'm sorry, but it will never be like that. Can you accept that?" I was as sincere and gentle with him as I could possibly be. It was killing me that I was breaking his heart.

He sat there quietly for a moment. "Well, I guess I have to, don't I? I can't make you feel something that you don't." He seemed so sad, turning his face away from mine.

The last thing I wanted to do was break Huck's heart. Unfortunately there was no way to keep from doing just that. It hurt me deeply to cause him such pain. Maybe one day he could forgive me and just be happy for Adam and me. I knew it would probably be a while until that happened though.

"We should probably go, don't you think?" I said, really wanting to end the conversation.

Huck looked outside at the weather, which had changed to a dull gray drizzle. It didn't appear that it was going to get much better the longer was sat there, so he agreed.

"I'll give you a ride home. You can't walk in this." Even after I just broke his heart in two, he was still so kind to me.

The ride home was silent and uncomfortable. Luckily it was a short ride back. I'm not sure what Huck expected to get out of telling me that he loved me. He had to know that I didn't feel the same way about him.

When we arrived back at the ranch, Huck walked me to the front door. Always the gentleman.

"Do you want to come in?" I said, hoping he would say no. After what he said to me in the library, we needed some time apart. I could tell that we were both feeling a bit uncomfortable.

"Um, no thanks. I have to get to work anyway. I have the evening shift." He turned and left.

Violet was sitting in the living room, sipping hot tea, and who knows what else, when I walked in. I didn't even notice her at first, as I walked over to sit on the couch and think about what had just happened. I did love Huck. He was my best friend. But, Adam was the one my heart wanted. As taboo as that was, it was the truth. There was nothing else in the world I wanted more than to be with Adam. I honestly didn't care that he was rich. His money wasn't important to me. He was. We could go work some lame jobs somewhere and live in a crappy apartment, eating bread and water for every meal, for all I cared. None of that mattered, as long as we were together. That's all I wanted in my life. I smiled at the thought of Adam leaving his posh life for some crappy apartment with me. I knew he loved me, but he would probably draw the line at that.

"What are you smiling about?" Violet startled me. I thought I was alone.

"Oh, hi," I said to her, when I looked up and saw her watching me. It was a little weird, she hadn't said a word until just then. It kind of gave me the creeps.

"Abigail." That was it. No 'hello' or anything. Just my name. It was just like her.

"Is there something going on between you and your little colored friend?" she asked me.

It only took a second to register what she had just said and I jumped up out of my seat. "My what? Oh my god, don't call him that!" I yelled at her.

She sighed heavily at that. She was clearly annoyed, but remained calm.

"Abigail, please, sit down. You are making a scene."

I looked around the room. "I'm making a scene? We are the only two people here."

"It's just an expression, Abigail. Besides, there are several people that live in this house. Anyone could overhear us at any time. So, please keep your voice down," she said calmly.

I didn't sit down as instructed. "My friend has a name. It's Huck. I would appreciate it if you would call him by his actual name when you talk about him, not that racist term. He is a person, and would prefer to be referred to as such." I was not backing down. It was important that she knew her hateful words were not okay with me.

"Really, don't be so dramatic. When I was growing up, that's what we called them. And this is my house, I'll say anything I want."

"Just because something was acceptable in the past, doesn't make it okay now." Maybe a gentler tactic would work on her. "I would really appreciate it if you didn't use that term when talking about my friend. Please." I was hopeful, eyes wide.

She paused, thinking for a moment. "Well, all right. I don't really know why I'm agreeing to anything. This is my house, after all. But, just to keep you calm, I will try to remember to not use that word around you."

A small victory perhaps, but I'll take it.

CHAPTER 16

Well, it happened. Despite my best efforts to the contrary, I found out I was pregnant. Stupid, stupid, stupid, were the only things that instantly came to my mind. I thought we were being careful, but obviously not careful enough. Violet's plan had worked, even though I had refused to play along. She would probably be thrilled, now that she was going to have an heir to the throne. I was terribly upset at first. Not quite sixteen years old, I was far too young to have a child. Maybe I should give the baby to Adam and Sarah, as Violet had originally planned. That would certainly solve the problem of trying to raise a child alone. I knew I wouldn't be able to stay working at the ranch, with Adam's bastard child in tow. Either I would have to leave while still pregnant, or give the baby to them. This was going to be one of the hardest decisions of my short life, and I was not really known for making good choices.

Adam needed to know, and I would tell him soon. But, I needed to tell someone else first.

I walked into the coffee house that afternoon and sat down at the table I hadn't been at for several weeks. That's how long it had been since Huck told me he loved me and I rejected him. At least that's the way he saw it. I spotted him over in the far corner having a heated conversation with someone that I couldn't see, because he had his back to me. When he moved a bit, I saw that it was Teresa. I had heard through the gossip mill, aka Oliver, that Huck and Teresa had started dating again, shortly after our last conversation. Their conversation now looked very serious.

Huck looked over his shoulder and spotted me sitting at the table. He then turned back around, said something to Teresa, and got up to go back over to the counter to help a customer. Teresa made a beeline for the front door, spotting me as she passed. Tears were streaming down her face. She didn't say a word to me, but if looks could kill...

When Huck finished ringing up the customer, he grabbed two cups of coffee and headed over to my table. We were the only two people in the place, except for the cook back in the kitchen.

"Hi," he said to me. "Mind if I sit down?" Without waiting for my answer, he sat down and handed me a cup of coffee.

"Hi back," I replied, taking the coffee.

"So what are you doing here? I didn't expect to see you again," he told me.

"I'm not angry with you, Huck. I figured you just needed some space, so I gave you some. Now I want us to be friends again. I miss you." I was sincere. I had missed him terribly. Life was very lonely without my best friend.

"I know. I miss you too. I acted like a jerk. You love Adam and I get that. It just hurt me and I needed some time. I'm glad you came in."

I jumped up out of my chair and gave him a big bear hug. I struggled to keep from crying. I was so happy to have him back. "You know I love you, right?" I asked him.

"Yeah, I know," he said softly.

"So what is up with you and Teresa?" I asked him. "Things looked pretty intense from over here."

"Oh, that. It's nothing. We started seeing each other again after…well, you know. But, I don't love her. I felt it was time to tell her that. I was just trying to be honest. She didn't take it very well."

"Yeah, I saw that. I hope you didn't bring my name up while you were breaking up with her. She gave me the stink eye as she was running out the door."

"No, of course not. I think she knows how I feel about you though. I probably wasn't very good at hiding it." He seemed a little embarrassed by that.

"Oh. Well, there is a reason I came to see you," I quickly changed the subject.

"I thought you came to see me because of my incredible handsomeness." He grinned.

He was very cute and that made me smile.

"Well, yes, of course there's that," I retorted. "But, there's more." It was fun joking around a bit with him again. I had missed him so much.

"I have news," was all I said.

"Okay." He leaned back in his chair, precariously balancing his coffee cup on his chest, waiting for me to continue.

I hesitated. How was I going to tell him? He would be devastated. Okay, here goes. "I'm pregnant." I kind of grimaced, bracing for the inevitable fight that was coming.

He just looked at me and said nothing.

"Aren't you going to say anything?" I asked him.

"Well, what do you want me to say? What's done is done. Me getting mad about it is not going to change anything, is it?" He sat his chair back down on all four legs and put his coffee cup on the table carefully.

"I guess not. This is just not the reaction I was expecting."

"So, what are you going to do now? How did Adam take it?" he asked.

"I haven't told Adam yet. I wanted you to know first. I was hoping you could help me sort this whole thing out. I have no idea what I'm going to do now. He's probably not going to take it very well." Obviously.

"You think? As much as I hate it, as much as I hate this whole thing, you have to tell Adam. He has a right to know." Huck told me matter-of-factly.

"I know he does. I'll tell him soon." I was putting it off as long as I could.

"What do you think he is going to say, when you do tell him?" Huck asked me.

"I'm not really sure. On the one hand, he will probably be happy, because Sarah can't have kids and I know he wants them. On the other hand, he is married and will have to deal with his wife finding out that he got me pregnant. At least I think so. He's got to tell her, right? Would he expect me to hide it from her?"

"Those are good questions. I barely know him and have no idea how he is going to react," Huck responded.

"I don't know how he is going to react either. I could see it going a variety of ways. I'm suddenly terrified of having a conversation with him about it."

I wasn't kidding either. With Sarah and Violet involved, who knew what the outcome would be. I really didn't want to go back home and face him, or any of them. So I stayed and hung out with Huck for a while, long after I was supposed to be back to work. Oh well, what was Oliver going to do about it? Nothing, that's for sure. Or would he? Would Adam let Oliver fire me now that I was carrying his child? Good question. I guess I was about to find out the answer to that.

****

Later that evening, Adam found me alone in the kitchen. Oliver had left for the day and I was just doing the final daily cleanup. I hadn't worked up the nerve to tell him yet.

"Abbey, can we talk?"

"Sure, about what?" I tried to sound light and breezy, without giving away my apprehension.

"Let's talk upstairs. I'll meet you there in five minutes."

I immediately went up to the third floor room with the Picasso in it. I called it "the love nest," though I don't think that amused Adam. This was the room where we usually met to be together without anyone knowing. Most of the staff didn't even know it existed, and we could lock it from the inside. We spent many wonderful hours in there, just being together. I got to know Adam like no one I had ever met before and I knew that he was the love of my life. It only took a couple of minutes until Adam showed up. When he walked in, he locked the door and we sat on the couch, facing each other. Something was definitely up. He was acting kind of strange, which made me start to worry. I suddenly got the feeling I was about to be dumped.

"I want to talk to you about something," he began. "I love you." He took both of my hands in his.

"I know."

"Okay, just wait. I'm not done yet." He seemed a bit irritated that I had interrupted him.

"Sorry. Go ahead."

"Like I said, I love you. You are the one I want to be with, not Sarah. I never really loved her, not in the way I should anyhow. You are the one I love. I want us to get married."

I think my heart skipped a beat when he said that. Wow, that was not what I was expecting at all. Just the opposite actually. But I was only excited for a few seconds.

I was skeptical. "How is that going to work? You know, the whole you already having a wife thing?"

"I'll divorce Sarah, and then after a respectful amount of time, we can get married. Will you?" He looked hopeful, raising his eyebrows in a questioning gaze.

I thought for a moment. Oh boy. This is exactly what I wanted. However, the next few minutes were going to be very important in determining my future. I had to tell him. How could I not?

"Well, there are two things that you need to know before we go any further in this conversation." I said, trying to remain calm. "Three things actually." I held up three fingers for emphasis.

"Okay, what?" He was definitely curious where this was all going.

"First, I love you too." I leaned over and kissed him passionately.

"I like where this is going," he said, smiling brightly.

"Second, I'm pregnant," I just blurted out, looking at him with a smile, hopeful that he wouldn't be furious at me.

"What? Oh my god, that's wonderful. I love you so much." He then leaned over and hugged me tight, then kissed me again. "I've always wanted children and Sarah couldn't have them. Oh sorry, I shouldn't bring her up right now. I don't want to spoil this. I'm not sure how we are going to work this all out, but we will find a way. I want us to be together, as a family." I could hear in his voice how excited he was and it made me smile.

Well, that was easy. Now the really hard part. I knew it was going to change everything, but there was no way around it. It was the most important and scariest thing of all. He had to know.

"There's one more thing," I told him.

"Oh yeah, I almost forgot. What is it?" He was still

beaming from the news.

I took a deep breath. "I'm 15 years old." There. I said it. He knew at last.

I watched as his face slowly changed from a wide grin to a deep frown, as the realization hit him.

"Oh crap," was all he could manage to say. It looked to me as if shock chased the breath from his lungs. He could hardly speak.

"I'm sorry that I lied. I needed the job and knew you would never hire me if you knew," I said quickly, before he had a chance to say anything else.

"I can't believe this. How could you not tell me you were 15 freaking years old!" he screamed at me.

He was furious and I couldn't blame him. I would not be surprised at all if he never talked to me again. I suddenly had visions of me being kicked to the curb and raising my baby out on the streets, alone and destitute.

"I'm sorry," I said quietly, not daring to look him in the eyes.

"You already said that. I can't believe this is happening. This is a nightmare. You know that I could go to jail for this?"

"I know. But, I won't let that happen. I wanted this as much as you do. We are in love, it will be okay." I tried to calm him down, patting him on the knee.

He pushed my hand away and scowled at me. "No one will care that you were willing or that we are in love. The fact is that I got a 15 year old pregnant. There is no way to talk my way out of this one." He bent his head down and put his hands on each side of his head, in deep thought. I thought he was going to start crying.

"We have to tell my mother," he said suddenly. "She will be furious, but hopefully will help us."

"Oh I don't think she'll be furious," I blurted out without thinking.

"What do you mean by that?" He looked at me, clearly confused by my comment.

Oops. "Oh, nothing. I just thought that maybe she would like to have a grandchild. I've heard her mention before that the house could use some children running around." I was just throwing anything out there that I could think of, hoping something might stick. He couldn't know about Violet's plan.

"Yeah, maybe. But, I doubt it. My mother is all about appearances. Me having a baby with you, and not my wife, will not be good for the family's reputation."

"Yeah, I guess."

This whole thing about appearances and reputations was completely ridiculous to me. People should be able to just live their lives and not spend it worrying about what people think. People should just be their authentic selves. I didn't want to spend my life trying to be something that I was not, just to make other people happy. Screw them.

"Let's get out of here. I want to think about this whole mess and I'll talk to you tomorrow. Okay?" he asked. He seemed a bit calmer.

"Okay."

I knew he need time to process everything. It was a lot for one afternoon. Now that he knew I was 15, I figured the wedding was off.

CHAPTER 17

The next morning Adam told me that he was going to go talk to his mother, alone.

"Wait, no. I think I should be there." I was terrified that Violet might say something about our non-existent plan and implicate me.

"I really think that I should talk to her without you. She will not be happy and having you there might make it worse."

"No it won't. We are in this together and I want to come with you. It's not fair for you to take all the heat yourself. I deserve to be yelled at too." I really meant that. This mess wasn't all on him. I was just as guilty.

His eyes looked to the side, deep in thought. "Well, okay, that's fine. Let's go now, before I lose my nerve."

We found Violet in the library with her usual cup of tea. We walked in and closed the door behind us. She looked up, surprised to see us together.

"Mother, we have something to talk to you about."

"Okay, sit down." She gestured toward the couch across from where she was sitting. We sat.

"I don't really know how to say this," he began. "But, here goes." He took a deep breath. "Abbey is pregnant and it's mine."

She didn't even miss a beat. "I see. What are your plans now?"

We both looked at her, not expecting such a calm reaction to the news. Well, I kind of expected it. Violet very much wanted me to get pregnant, but Adam didn't know that, obviously.

"Why are you so calm about this? Did you hear what I said?" he asked her.

"Yes, I heard you. What is the point in getting upset now? What's done is done. Now we have to figure out what to do about it." She was still very serene. Would it have hurt her to at least act a bit surprised and angry about it? A little acting would have gone a long way. Adam didn't seem to notice though.

"Well, you might not be so calm after this next bit of information," He continued. "She's 15 years old," he said much more quietly.

"Almost 16." I volunteered, like that really made any difference.

With that, she was definitely taken aback. "She's 15? Why didn't anyone tell me this?!" There it was. Now she was agitated.

"I just found out myself," was Adam's response, while giving me a sideways glance.

I suddenly felt betrayed. Please, not now.

"It's all my fault. I wanted this job so much, that I lied to everyone. Adam didn't know until yesterday," I interjected.

"What in the world are we going to do now?" she asked. She was clearly upset, knowing full well what the implications of my being 15 years old meant for Adam and his future.

"We want to get married. After I divorce Sarah, of course," Adam told her. He was much more forceful then.

"Absolutely not." Violet was very direct and it sounded a lot like it was not up to debate. "Sarah is a better wife for you and I won't have this gutter snake as a daughter-in-law. What would people think?"

"Mother!" Adam yelled, jumping up off the couch. "Don't call her that! I love her, and she is going to be the mother of your grandchild." He was standing over Violet as he said it. It didn't seem to phase her at all.

"Really Adam, sit down. Your hysterics are not helping." She then calmly took a sip of her tea.

She obviously was not going to engage in a fight with him, so he sat back down on the couch, next to me. He looked over at me and said he was sorry that his mother called me that. Violet heard him and did not respond. The woman was cool under pressure.

"Now, about her age. Who else knows?" Violet asked Adam directly.

I answered back. "No one. You are the only two people here that know." I didn't mention that Huck and Teresa also knew. They wouldn't tell anyone.

"Good. No one else needs to know. Do I make myself clear?" She was looking directly at me.

"As glass," I responded.

"You two will stop seeing each other immediately," she announced.

"No we won't," Adam told her. He looked at me and smiled. "She's pregnant with my child. Whether she's 15 or not, I want to be with her."

"We will discuss that more later." And that was the end of that topic, apparently.

"Now, let's move on. Does Sarah know about the baby?" she asked Adam.

"No, not yet," Adam told her.

"Well, you need to go tell her right now, without Abigail there to make things worse."

"Yes, you're right. I'll go now. Come on Abbey."

Adam and I got up to leave.

"Actually, Abigail, I would like you to stay. I would like to speak with you alone," she said.

Adam and I looked at each other. He nodded for me to stay. I couldn't believe he did that. Did he not know his mother at all? She was going to tear me a new one as soon as he walked out the door. I gave him a look and walked over and sat down. Boy, was he ever going to pay for that later. Of course, I knew he had it worse than I did. He was the one that had to tell his wife that he got someone else pregnant. That was going to be the toughest conversation of his life. I felt a bit sorry for him. I wished that I could be there for moral support, but I knew that would just make matters worse. They needed to have that talk alone.

"Close the door behind you, Adam," Violet called after him.

Once he was out and the door was closed, she started in on me. "So, I thought you were going to be careful and not get yourself pregnant?" She was very smug.

"I didn't get myself pregnant. There were two of us involved." I was in no mood to put up with her smart ass comments. I had Adam on my side to help deal with her.

"You are an idiot for not taking me up on my offer." Wow, no holding anything back with this woman. "Now you are doing it for free."

Well, she had me there. Maybe I should have taken her up on her offer. That way, I would have gotten Adam, had his baby, like I am now, and get a nice chunk of money for the rest of my life. Not now though. Maybe I was an idiot. If that was the case, and it certainly seemed to be, at least I can be honest with Adam, because the truth is that I did love him and didn't mind having his baby. I was going to keep it though. I was not giving it to Adam and Sarah, so that his mother could be an influence to the child. I couldn't have that. Violet would ruin him or her. I loved Adam, but he was kind of a mess when it came to his mother. He had no backbone at all. I wanted my child to grow up strong and independent, not under the rule of Violet Tyler.

"I'm not doing it for free. Adam and I are going to get married and raise the baby together. I don't need your money." God, I hoped that was the case.

"Don't be absurd. Adam talks a big game, but in the end he will never marry you. Adam will never leave Sarah for you. I'm not even worried about that."

She almost seemed to be mocking me. It was painfully obvious that she was telling the truth, she wasn't worried about me at all. Did she really have that big of a hold over him? Would he abandon me, and our baby, for Sarah? He told me himself that he never really loved Sarah like a wife. He said I was the one that he loved. I know he was telling the truth. If not, then he is the world's best liar, because I believed every word he said. He even stuck up for me to his mother. That had to prove how much he loved me. Violet was not an easy woman to defy.

"Besides," she continued, "if he ever found out that you did agree to seduce him and get pregnant on purpose, even though you tried to back out, he would hate you." She smiled at that one and it sounded a lot like a threat.

Before I had a chance to respond, the door to the library burst open and Adam came storming in. He had a look of fury on his face.

"Are you serious?" He was taking long, quick strides directly toward me. "You planned this whole thing?" He stopped only a few inches in front of me. I could see the anger in his eyes. They were cold and hard. It was a bit scary.

"What? Where did you come from? What did you hear?" I was suddenly terrified of what he had overheard.

"I heard it all. About how you and my mother planned it all." He looked over at his mother and back to me. "How could you do this?" He seemed more hurt by the fact that I betrayed him than his mother betraying him.

"No, you don't understand. We didn't plan it…" I tried to explain, but he interrupted me.

"Just stop right there." He put his palm up toward me. "I heard everything. You can't deny it now. I can't believe you did this! Either one of you." He backed up a bit then, so he could see both of us together. I don't think I have ever seen him so angry.

"How did your talk with Sarah go?" I think this was Violet's misguided attempt to change the subject a bit and calm him down.

"I haven't talked to her yet. I was listening to your conversation through the door." He didn't seem sorry one bit about eavesdropping.

"Adam, I love you. It's not what you think," I tried to explain. As I reached for his arm to calm him down, he jerked it away from me.

"I don't believe you. I don't believe anything you have to say. You've been lying to me all this time! We are through. I will never forgive you for this," he said through clenched teeth in a very aggressive, and scary way.

Adam then turned and walked out. I started to follow him, but he turned on me abruptly. "Don't you dare come after me."

I stopped in my tracks and covered my face, crying. For a while I had someone in the house that was on my side, someone that loved me even when it felt like everyone around hated me. Now all of that was gone. Adam walked out without another word. My betrayal was something that we might never recover from.

"Now look what you have done," Violet started in on me.

"What I have done? You did this. This thing is entirely your fault. You need to explain to him that I did not agree to any of this stupid plan with you." I meant it, too.

"I will do no such thing. And now you are carrying my grandchild. You better not dare leave this house with that baby."

"Just get away from me!" I screamed, running from the room.

I ran all the way to my room, threw myself on my bed and cried for an hour. At one point, Oliver sent one of the maids to look for me and I told her I was not feeling well and would not be in to work. He would just have to get over it. I knew he wouldn't, or couldn't, fire me. They wouldn't voluntarily throw me out of the house while I was pregnant with their heir. In a few months, that might be a different story though. Until then, I felt like I was pretty safe.

CHAPTER 18

"Adam told me about the baby," Sarah hissed at me the next morning while I was clearing the breakfast dishes from the dining room table.

She had stayed behind after everyone went on about their day. Before she even said anything, I figured that she knew, by the way she was glaring at me all through breakfast. It made me very nervous and my hands started to shake. At one point I almost dropped an armload of dishes and food I was carrying, but Adam jumped up and saved the entire haul, at the last possible moment. I tried to thank him, but he ignored me and sat back down. He was not going to forgive me anytime soon. After serving everyone I went back to the kitchen to calm down. Finally everyone was gone, except Sarah. Oh goody.

"I see." It was the only thing I said in response to her declaration.

There was no point in arguing with her about it. She had a right to be angry and I had no defense on my part. I didn't think that telling her I was in love with her husband was going to help. Maybe if I kept my mouth shut, she might calm down some.

I walked into the kitchen and put an armload of dishes in the sink. She stayed in the other room and I really hoped she would be gone when I went back in for the rest of the dishes. No such luck. As I walked back into the dining room, she stood up and started following me around.

"Is that all you have to say for yourself?" she asked

me. It was obvious she was angry. I expected that. I would be, if I were her.

"I really don't know what else to say. I'm sorry?" I looked back at her nervously, since she was right on my heels.

"Is that a question? Are you asking me if you are sorry?" she snapped.

I stopped and turned around to face her. "No. I'm really sorry. It was stupid and I hurt you. I had no right to do that." I meant it too. I was the one in the wrong, not Sarah.

"No you didn't. Adam is my husband and he will never leave me for you." She sounded very confident of that.

"I know." I replied, looking down at my feet in shame. She was right. He would never leave her for me. Violet would not let that happen.

"What do you plan to do now?" she asked.

"I guess I'm going to have a baby."

She looked even angrier then, her expression tight. "You don't need to get smart with me. You know what I mean. Are you planning to raise this baby alone?"

"I really don't know what I'm going to do yet. I have to talk to Adam about it."

I started walking away from her, back toward the kitchen, when she grabbed me by the arm and stopped me. She whirled me around to face her, causing me to drop the dishes in my hands. We both looked down at the mess. Just great, more work for me.

"I don't think so. You are not to have anymore

conversations with Adam alone. All conversations will include me from now on. Got it?"

"Yeah, I got it." I jerked my arm away from her and walked back to the kitchen with another load of dishes. I left the mess on the floor for the time being. I didn't want to be in the room alone with Sarah any longer than I needed to be. When I returned, she was gone. Thank goodness.

About an hour later I heard Adam and Sarah arguing viciously. They were in the library, with the door closed, but it really didn't help much. They were screaming. Even though they were so loud, their words were mostly muffled by the books, walls and doors. It wasn't really my intention to try to listen, but I found myself standing outside the door anyway. I could pick out a few words here and there. I heard my name a few times, and I heard Violet's name too. I didn't really know what Violet had to do with any of this. I'm sure Sarah had no idea what Violet had been plotting, but around that house, you never knew what was going on. There were so many lies and such deceit, I just didn't know what to think anymore. I wondered if Adam told Sarah about Violet's plan. He wouldn't dare tell her, would he? There was no reason for him to now. I was already pregnant, so why get his mother all wrapped up in this if he didn't need to? It was his mother though, and they were very close, so who knows.

The fight was obviously about me and the baby. So, I had to listen in. After about ten minutes of standing there eavesdropping, I saw Oliver heading toward me in the hall and I turned around and took off the other way. I know he saw me, but I ran anyway. What a coward I was.

For the next couple of days I didn't even see Sarah, and Adam seemed to vanish quickly whenever we ended up in the same room together. I guess everyone was avoiding me. Boy, this was going to be a really long seven or so months. Wow, only seven months to figure out what I was going to do. That kind of seemed like a long time to figure something out, but it really wasn't. This was a decision that was going to affect the rest of my life. Would I have the baby and raise it alone, with no help from anyone? Would Adam send me money? Would Sarah even let him help? Would Adam come visit the baby? Would he leave her for me? Doubtful. But, in my mind there was always hope. Maybe he would come around and realize again that I was the one for him, not Sarah. He didn't love her like he loved me. I knew that. I just needed him to know that. He did a few days ago, but now he was so angry with me, because of Violet, that he wouldn't even be in the same room with me. I hated Violet for that. She caused all of these problems. If it weren't for her, Adam and I would be together now, happy and in love, expecting our first child. At least in my head that is the way it would have all worked out. In reality? I don't think I'll ever know. I seriously doubted that Adam would come around, unless Violet told him the truth, and I couldn't fathom that happening in any way whatsoever.

****

"Can I talk to you?" Adam startled me in the

stables and I flinched. I had been brushing one of the horses and was lost in thought.

"Oh, I didn't hear you walk up. What do you want to talk about?" I was encouraged that he wanted to talk to me at all.

He looked around to make sure that no one was within earshot. He even went so far as to look in every single stall, which took several minutes. I just stood there, wondering what in the world was so secretive that he was terrified of anyone hearing.

"Maybe we should go for a walk, away from prying ears," he said, looking around nervously.

"Adam, I've been in here for half an hour alone. No one is here. What do you want to talk about?" I was getting impatient.

"Well, okay." He still looked very nervous, while rubbing the back of his neck.

"Sarah, my mother, and I all had a talk about you."

"I'm sure you did. Can't wait to hear how that turned out," I answered back, sarcastically.

He seemed to overlook my sarcasm and continued what he was saying.

"Sarah and I would like to raise the baby together." He seemed apprehensive when saying it, and just stood there waiting for me to respond.

"What? Are you kidding me? You are kidding, right?" I didn't know how else to respond to what he just said. My heart began to race with fear and worry. "This can't be true. Where will I be in all of this?" I was afraid to ask.

"Well, you won't be anywhere. We will be raising the baby, not you."

"This was your mother's idea, wasn't it?" I was becoming agitated.

"Well..I guess. I mean, she brought it up, but we both liked the idea. Why does it matter anyway?"

"Wait, let me see if I got this right. I stay here, have your baby and then leave so Sarah can adopt it? Is that about right?" I was starting to get a bit freaked out.

"Well…not exactly." He hesitated while saying it.

"What is that supposed to mean?"

"We want to have the baby together. Sarah and I. We want everyone to think she is pregnant with my child, not you."

When he said that, my head started spinning. I started seeing stars and felt faint. I reached instinctively for a chair, so I wouldn't fall. But we were in the stables and there wasn't one within reach. As everything went black, I saw Adam lunge toward me and grab me, just as my knees gave way.

CHAPTER 19

When I woke up, I was in the parlor on the first floor, laying on the couch. Everyone was standing over me. And I mean everyone. I think the entire family and every single servant, as well as a few ranch hands were packed into the room, staring. Sarah was kneeling beside me, taking my blood pressure.

"You're pressure is fine," she told me, standing back up.

With all the people gathered around me, I felt like they were depleting all the oxygen in the room. I started breathing quickly, trying to get some air. I thought sitting up might help. As I I tried to sit up, Adam leaned over and put his hand behind my back to help me. At that moment, I looked up to see Sarah glaring at him. Adam saw her too and abruptly let go of me, causing me to almost fall onto the floor. But, I righted myself, no thanks to him.

"What is going on?" I asked, just a little confused. I hadn't completely gotten my senses back and didn't quite remember the scene in the stables.

"You fainted," Adam told me.

I thought for just a moment. "Oh yeah, that's right. I'm fine. Everyone can go now." I was a bit embarrassed by all the people standing over me.

"Everyone out!" shouted Violet, waving her arms as they all dispersed in short order. Only Adam, Sarah and Violet remained. The room went from dozens of voices to very quiet almost instantly. It was unnerving.

"Are you all right?" Adam asked me, looking very concerned as he kneeled beside me.

"Yes, I said I'm fine." I tried to stand up again.

"Please stay where you are. We'd like to talk to you," Sarah said, sounding almost pleasant. I sat back down and she sat on the couch next to me.

"Okay," Sarah continued, "I know that Adam tried to explain to you what we wanted, but clearly did not do a very good job at it." She gave him another one of her looks.

"Oh no, Adam told me exactly what you want. It's the same thing Violet has been trying to get me to do for months."

With that, we all turned to look at Violet. She just shrugged her shoulders. "I was just trying to help," she told us. The innocent act was not working on me.

"Look, Abbey, you are in no position to raise a baby and we are," Adam told me. He was right about that. "We can give it a good home, a family, a great education, anything he or she needs. You won't be able to do that."

I thought about what he said. He made some really good points. I was not quite sixteen years old, about to have a baby, and had no plan whatsoever. I had nowhere to live, no money, no husband, nothing. I couldn't think of a good argument to that, so I didn't respond.

Then Sarah jumped back in. "It may sound strange to you, but if I'm going to raise this baby, I want everyone to think it's mine. I don't want to have to explain constantly why I'm raising a child that my husband had with another woman. People would not understand and he or she wouldn't be accepted the way our child together would. You don't want that for your child, do you?" she asked me. She seemed to be holding her breath while waiting for an answer from me.

"No, not really." I couldn't argue with her. She was probably right. All I wanted was for my child to be happy and healthy, even if that meant I was not the one to raise him or her. "I need to think about it. Can we talk about this later?"

"Of course." Adam responded. "Sarah said you are okay, so you can go. Do you want me to walk you to your room?" He looked quickly over at Sarah when he asked me that.

"I'll take her," Violet chimed in.

She kind of pushed her way in between Adam and me, and took my arm to walk me toward my room. While on the way, she couldn't resist the urge to give me her opinion on the whole situation.

"Abigail, I know this must be very difficult for you, but this really is the best solution for all involved."

"Is it?" I asked her.

"Of course. Do you want to raise your child alone out on the streets? Because that is what is going to happen. Adam will not be supporting this child, if he is not the one raising it. I will see to that." I could tell by her tone that she certainly meant business.

"I think Adam can decide that for himself." I regretted saying it the instant it came out of my mouth.

"Have you not met me?" she retorted. I got the point.

Just then we reached my room and I stopped just inside the door. I didn't want her following me in.

"My, I had forgotten how sad these little rooms are," she said, looking past me, taking in the room. "It's been years since I've been in this part of the house. We will talk in the morning," she said as she turned and walked away.

God, I hated that woman. She was the most horrible, nasty person I had ever met. And, that is saying a lot, after my background as a drug addict. I have certainly met some vile people, but Violet was the worst. I wouldn't wish her on my worst enemy.

****

The next morning, very early, when the sunlight was just starting to peek in between the slats of the blinds on my window, came a knock at my bedroom door. It wasn't a quiet, timid knock either. You know, the kind of knock someone makes when they know you are probably asleep, but want to wake you anyway? No, it wasn't that. It was a loud, almost pounding noise against the door. It startled me and I sat up quickly in bed.

"What?" I said groggily, while rubbing the sleep out of my eyes.

"It's Adam and Sarah. We need to talk to you." It was Adam's voice on the other side of the door.

"What? Why?" I still wasn't fully awake. "What's the matter?"

"It's about the baby," he kind of whispered loudly, if there is such a thing.

Were they serious? "I'm going to be pregnant for several more months. I'm sure this can wait until breakfast!" I yelled back, hoping everyone would hear me.

It was quiet on the other side of the door for a full minute. I could kind of hear them talking in a whisper, but couldn't quite make out what they were saying. I laid back down and started to doze back off, when Adam started talking again, waking me back up. Jeez, can't a girl get any sleep in this house?

"Fine, Abbey. We will talk to you at breakfast."

I didn't even bother answering as I heard them walk away. There would be plenty of time for talking later and I fell back asleep quickly.

A couple of hours later, I was serving breakfast to them in the small dining room, like I did most mornings, when Sarah asked me to sit down. She definitely wasn't inviting me to have breakfast with them. Heaven forbid. She just wanted me to sit, so I sat. She looked around to make sure there were no prying ears nearby. It was just Adam and Sarah for breakfast, no Violet, which was very unusual. She ate breakfast with them almost every morning.

"As you can see, Violet is not here today," Sarah said. I'm pretty sure she was not expecting a response. "We wanted to talk to you about this whole situation without her here."

"Okay."

"We know that you are young and really can't raise

a baby on your own."

"Didn't we already cover this yesterday?" I asked her. It was getting old listening to everyone tell me how young and incapable I was.

"Yes," Sarah continued. "But we had a long talk about this last night, just the two of us, without his mother," she said, looking over at Adam.

So far, Adam had not said a word. He was letting Sarah do all the talking.

"And I know that you and Adam are not on the best of terms right now." She sounded almost sincere. "That's why I'm here to help."

"Okay." I had such a way with words.

"Anyway, we want to offer you some money to help you get back on your feet after you have the baby."

It took me a moment and then it hit me. "Wait, you want me to sell my baby to you?" I asked her.

"No. No, of course not," Adam finally jumped in. "We want you to give us the baby, and we want to just help you out."

"That sounds a lot like baby selling to me!" I yelled, jumping up out of my seat. "This was Violet's idea, wasn't it?"

"No, why would you say that? She has nothing to do with this," Adam said.

"Because Violet already tried that and it didn't work. What makes you think you can talk me into it if she couldn't?"

"She did what?" Adam asked me. "Why is this the

first time I'm hearing about this?"

His eyes went wide and he looked really scared that I would blow his cover. He obviously already knew. He and I had a big blow up about it after he heard me and Violet talking about it. But, I played along. Maybe it would help me score some points with him. What did I have to lose? He already hated me. It couldn't get any worse.

"Probably because I told her there was no way I would do that," I said, and was starting to get very agitated.

"When did this happen?" Sarah asked. She looked like she was starting to put the pieces together.

"It was before Adam and I even started seeing each other. She wanted me to seduce Adam and get pregnant on purpose. She said she needed an heir and you couldn't provide that," I blurted out without thinking.

"What?!" Sarah yelled this time, jumping up out of her chair.

Oh crap. What have I done?

CHAPTER 20

"Okay calm down," Adam told Sarah, taking her hand and urging her to sit back down.

Sarah sat back down and wouldn't look at me, keeping her eyes lowered. She looked like she was about to cry.

"How could you do this? How could you sleep with my husband and get pregnant?" She was deeply hurt. I could see it on her face.

At that moment, I finally got it. I finally understood what I had done to her. Sarah had married the man she loved, the man she planned to spend the rest of her life with, maybe have a houseful of children, and grow old together. Then I came along and screwed everything up. I had no right to do that. He belonged to her, not to me. Now I was having his child and she wasn't. Of course she was hurt. Who wouldn't be? I felt like such a terrible person.

"I'm really very sorry. We can't help it that we fell in love," I told her. In my 15 year old mind, that was an apology.

Sarah looked me straight in the eyes then. "Fell in love? What are you talking about?" She looked over at Adam. "You told me it was just a couple of times. Did you lie to me about that too?"

Adam glared at me and then turned to Sarah. "Sweetheart, maybe we should talk about this in private." He took her hand and tried to gently get her to stand up and leave the room with him. She jerked her hand free and didn't budge from her chair. He sat back down.

"I don't want to talk about this in private. Everyone has been lying to me and it's time that I know the truth. All of it. About everything." She looked back and forth between Adam and me.

I was tired of the lies too and decided it was time to come clean.

"Everything I've told you is the truth," I said. "Violet came to me and tried to get me to seduce Adam and get pregnant. I told her no. Then Adam and I started seeing each other anyway, and fell in love. Well, I fell in love anyway. I can't say for sure if he was in love or not. You will have to ask him that."

We both looked at Adam then and he lowered his eyes in shame. He wasn't about to admit anything to either one of us at that moment. Any answer he gave was going to get him into a lot of trouble. He couldn't win.

I continued. "Either way, that's obviously not the case now. We have no relationship at all anymore. Anyhow, I got pregnant on accident. I did not plan it. We did not plan it together. Violet had nothing to do with our relationship, no matter how hard she tried to manipulate me and no matter how much she wants to take credit for it." I took a deep breath. "That's pretty much it."

"I see," she said, nodding.

It appeared to me that she believed me. Though I'm sure that she was still very hurt and very angry about the whole thing, she seemed calmer about it all of a sudden.

"Well, there's nothing we can do about this now. You are pregnant, that's a fact, and we all need to figure out what to do about that. Adam and I will deal with the rest of it in private. So, we want to go back to where this conversation started and ask you to give us the baby." She looked at me, with big eyes and hope written all over her face.

I knew that I had no business raising a baby on my own. I wasn't currently doing drugs, but knew that I might not be able to stay off of them forever. I vowed to stay clean, but just didn't know if it was possible. Drugs were a constant threat in my life. I was at least smart enough to know that I didn't want my baby mixed up in all that. I was starting to see the wisdom in giving my baby a better life than I could offer him or her. And I didn't want a baby, not really. Not now at least. One day probably, but not now. I was far too young and knew it.

"Are you sure that's what you want?" I was actually surprised that she would want to raise the love child of her husband and his mistress.

"Yes. Definitely," Adam chimed in. They both had a look of desperation on their faces.

I took a deep breath and let it out slowly. "Okay, I'll do it." I almost regretted it the second those words left my lips.

Both Adam and Sarah jumped up out of their seats and hugged me. I started to cry. They both sat back down and tried to console me. I think they knew how hard this decision was for me. Adam left for a couple of minutes to get me some water and tissues. When he returned, I found out the rest of the plan.

"There's something else we have to talk to you about," Adam said.

"Like what? What else could there possibly be? I'm going to let you adopt my baby and probably never see it again. Isn't that enough?" I just didn't need anymore surprises.

"We want everyone to think that I'm the one having the baby." She kind of grimaced when she said that, like she was terrified of my reaction. "I want to pretend that I'm pregnant. We want everyone we know to think this is actually our baby, not one that we adopted."

"I see. Didn't we already talk about this?" I asked them. "Exactly how is that going to work?"

"Well, yes, but we didn't get a straight answer. We haven't really worked out all the details yet, but you will stay in the house until the baby is born. There's probably no way to hide the fact that you are pregnant from the staff, but maybe you can tell them that you have a boyfriend in town and it's his. I would be pretending to be pregnant at the same time, so no one should catch on," Sarah told me.

It sure sounded to me like they had it all worked out already, even making up a fake boyfriend for me. Who would catch on anyway? It was such a ridiculous plan that no one would ever think that's what was going on.

"Okay, whatever. I guess it doesn't really matter to me if people think you gave birth to the baby. I will be leaving afterward and won't be around anyway. I do have one condition, though. Violet can't be in charge of anything regarding the baby. I don't want her influencing his or her life in any way whatsoever."

"Deal," they both said at the same time. They looked at each other and smiled, then looked at me. They seemed a bit embarrassed that this made them so happy and me so miserable.

And miserable I was. I went immediately to my room and cried for hours. I cried for my baby, but mostly for myself. I would never know my own child. I would never see him or her grow up, become an adult and have children of their own. Yes, I would probably have more children, but I knew in my heart that I would always love and long for this child. He or she would never leave my heart.

I refused to leave my room for days. Oliver sent a couple of the housekeepers to fetch me, but I wouldn't budge. I didn't care if he was angry at me or not. I knew that he couldn't fire me. I would go back to work when I was good and ready. Even Adam came to my room to see if I was okay. I told him I didn't want to talk to anyone and he gave me my space. At least he was considerate enough to have Oliver make me a tray three times a day and send it to my room. I'm sure Oliver was furious at that. He had no idea what was going on with me and probably didn't understand why no one fired me. They would certainly do that to him if he were acting the way I was acting. But, none of that mattered to me. I was safe for several more months. I could pretty much get away with anything I wanted. No one was going to get rid of me while I was carrying the heir to the fortune.

When I finally decided to venture out from my room, I went directly into town to see Huck. I knew his schedule and timed my visit perfectly to the end of his shift. He hugged me tight when he saw me standing outside waiting for him.

"So, I told Adam about the baby," I said as we started walking down the street, with no destination in mind.

"How did he take it?"

"He was really excited at first, until I told him I was only 15 years old. That freaked him out."

"Yeah, I'm sure it did. Does Sarah know?"

"She knows."

He didn't respond for a minute. He did seem like he had something on his mind though.

"So, I've been thinking," he started.

"About what?"

"About the baby. And about us. I know you are in love with Adam, but that's probably not going to happen. He's married, and you even said that he probably won't leave his wife."

"Yeah, I know. So, what's your point?" He really didn't need to rub it in.

"My point is that I still love you. I want us to be a family. You, me, and the little one. I have a job and can support us. I love kids and would be a great dad." He seemed so sincere.

"I know you would. But I can't. We can't. I'm not going to keep the baby." I almost started crying, but took a deep breath and calmed myself. Getting emotional now was not going to make this any easier.

"What is that supposed to mean? Are you getting rid of the baby? Please don't do that." He seemed very upset by that.

"No. No, of course not. I would never do that," I replied.

"Then what are you talking about?"

Oh boy, how in the world was I going to explain all of this mess to him? His offer was almost tempting, but I couldn't do that to him. I didn't love him and it wouldn't be fair. He didn't need a girl that didn't love him and a baby complicating his life. He needed to be free to find his own true love. I owed him that much.

At that moment, I noticed a cop and a young man, maybe 19 or 20, walking toward us. The cop wasn't wearing a uniform, but I saw his badge and gun under his suit jacket. I turned my head so he wouldn't see my face. I really had no idea if my parents had the cops looking for me or not, but I didn't want to take any chances.

"Huck, how have you been?" the cop said, as he passed. He never slowed down, continuing to walk past us.

"Hi detective. I'm fine. Thank you."

That was the end of the conversation. The young man with him never said a word. He did glare at Huck as they passed though, and it was definitely a hateful glare.

"What was that all about?" I asked Huck, once they

were out of earshot.

"Nothing. What do you mean?"

"How do you know that detective? And who was that with him?"

"That was just my friend, Sam Perez, and his dad. Sam is an ex-friend actually. We used to be friends, but got in a big fight over a girl, and now we aren't friends. That's pretty much it."

"That must be why he glared at you as he walked by."

"I don't really know why he's mad at me. He's still dating the girl, so he won. He has no reason to hate me. But, whatever. I don't want to talk about him. I want to talk about you and the baby."

"Oh, okay."

I spent the next few minutes telling him about my plan with Adam and Sarah. He didn't like it at all, but it was not his choice. He told me that he was going to spend the next few months trying to change my mind. He could try, but it wouldn't work. I had made up my mind.

CHAPTER 21

The next morning I got up bright and early and reported to work in the kitchen. Oliver was shocked that I actually showed up. He made some snide comment about it being nice that I decided to make an appearance. I ignored him and set about my day.

That afternoon, right after I finished cleaning up after lunch, the doorbell rang. Normally I didn't answer the door, but I was walking by, so I went ahead and opened the door. It was a delivery of several large boxes for Sarah. I signed for them, then noticed what they were: a crib, dresser and changing table. It was just too much and I ran to my room before anyone noticed how visibly upset I was.

Over the next few days, Sarah told everyone she knew that they were expecting. She didn't keep the 'good news' from anyone that would listen. I heard her tell them all about their plans for the new baby and the nursery they were setting up and names they were thinking of. My name never entered the conversation, not that I expected it to. It was just that I seemed to be completely forgotten. Neither Sarah nor Adam so much as looked my way when I was serving them their meals, or passed them in the hall. But, Violet gave me 'knowing looks.' I was actually surprised that she didn't gloat my way. That was fine with me.

The fewer the people that knew about the whole sordid mess, the better. At that point, only Adam, Sarah, Violet, and Huck knew the truth.

A couple of days later, my sixteenth birthday came

and went, without even a mention. I'm sure no one at the ranch had any idea it was my birthday and it really made me miss my parents. They would have made such a big deal about it. It was one of the saddest days of my life and I spent the day in my room sulking.

Over the next few months, I started to show and just explained to the staff that I was pregnant with my boyfriend's baby. I got a few raised eyebrows, but no one made any comments about it to my face. I never left the ranch the entire time. Adam and Sarah didn't want anyone outside the ranch to know I was pregnant. I'm not really sure why. It wasn't like anyone was going to figure out that Sarah was faking her pregnancy and I was going to give them my baby. Wow, the whole thing sounded completely ludicrous when I thought about it. Sarah, on the other hand, had no problem running around all over town, talking to people about the baby on the way, with her fake belly getting bigger and bigger.

They did offer me a good chunk of money to keep my mouth shut. I figured I was going to need it once the baby was born. There was no way they would let me keep my job after that. It would be weird anyway for me to be working at the house with my child there, being raised by someone else. That would never work. I wasn't really a prisoner, but it certainly felt that way. I couldn't even go into town to see Huck. He did come by a few times to see me, but he didn't feel very welcome and didn't stay long.

"You really need to get away from this house and these people," Huck told me one day, when we were sitting in the garden.

"They gave me a lot of money to stay here and give them the baby. I can't leave."

"Yes you can. What are they going to do? Call the cops? No, that wouldn't happen. They have basically bought your baby from you and that is completely illegal. They would never go to the cops. So, you don't owe them anything. You and I can leave together. Just give them the money back, if you want. We will be fine without it."

"Have you forgotten that this is Adam's baby too? It's not like I'm giving it to complete strangers. He is the father after all. And, as much as I don't like Sarah, I have to admit that I think she will be a good mother. She seems really excited to be getting this baby. Besides, I made a commitment to them and I plan to stick by my word. I can't raise a child anyway." I was so tired of having to defend my actions to everyone at the house. I shouldn't have to defend myself to Huck also.

"But I would be helping you. You don't have to do this alone," he pleaded.

"Please, Huck, stop harassing me about this. I'm not going to change my mind. What's done is done." I had had enough. I got up and walked into the house, leaving him sitting there on the bench in the garden. He didn't follow me.

"Abbey," Sarah cornered me in the hall as soon as she saw me walk in, "I'm having a few friends over tomorrow for a baby shower. I want everything to be perfect and have already given the refreshments list to

Oliver. Please make sure that everything goes smoothly." It wasn't a request, but more of a demand.

"Of course."

The next morning, Oliver and I set about making the food and drinks for her baby shower. I couldn't believe that she was having me do all the work for the baby shower she was throwing for my baby, while she was lying to everyone around her about it. But, I had agreed to the situation at hand, so what was I going to say about it?

Twelve women showed up to the baby shower. Honestly I didn't know there were even twelve people that liked her enough to come. Apparently I was wrong. Violet was conspicuously absent. Perhaps she didn't see any need to go to a baby shower when Sarah wasn't even pregnant. While everyone was settling in, I served the drinks. Everyone had alcohol, except Sarah. She needed to keep appearances up. By the time the food arrived, everyone was a bit sloshy. As I served the food, one of them noticed I was pregnant.

"So, I see that you are pregnant as well. Aren't you a bit young?" some short, squat blonde woman said to me. I didn't know anyone's name.

"I guess." That's all I wanted to say about it.

Then another one chimed in. "Are you married?" Man they could be nosey and the tone of her voice was very judgmental.

"It's not really any of your business," I told her.

Then I looked over at Sarah and she glared at me.

"She has a boyfriend. He works in town. They plan

to move out of the area as soon as the baby is born," Sarah told everyone.

I had no idea if she was just winging it, or if she had this story concocted all along in case someone asked. I still thought it was none of their business.

"Wow, you would think that girls today were smart enough not to get themselves knocked up. But, I guess not." This came from the short, squatty one again, and everyone laughed.

I felt my face get warm and I'm sure I turned a bright shade of red. Just as I started to give her a piece of my mind, Sarah jumped in.

"Abbey, why don't you bring in that delicious lemon cake that Oliver made?"

I knew what she was doing. I let her have her way and I started toward the kitchen. "I just have to frost it and will be back in a few minutes."

I walked directly to the bathroom in the back hall. That is where I knew there was a bottle of Ipecac. I grabbed it from the medicine cabinet and put it in my apron pocket, so no one would see me with it. When I got back to the kitchen, Oliver told me he was going to take a quick break and would be back in five minutes. I had to hurry. As soon as he walked out the door, I poured the contents of the bottle into the bowl of frosting. I then added a bit more sugar to help cover up any bad taste.

Once I finished frosting the cake, I cut it up and took a slice to everyone, even Sarah. It wouldn't hurt her since she wasn't actually pregnant. Everyone dug in immediately. I went back into the kitchen. If I had just stood there watching, waiting for something to happen, it would have looked a bit suspicious. I knew that it wouldn't take long before I was very aware of the outcome.

Roughly ten or fifteen minutes later I heard Sarah yell my name from the parlor. It was a desperate sort of sound, so I went in to see what she wanted, bracing myself for the inevitable. When I walked in, I couldn't help but smile to myself. I had to try really hard not to burst out laughing. Almost everyone at the party was holding her stomach and gagging. Many had already made a beeline for a bathroom. There were two of the women that seemed fine. When I looked at their plates, they had only taken a couple of small bites of the lemon cake. I guess it wasn't enough to hurt them.

"What have you done?!" Sarah screamed at me.

I looked at her like I had no idea what she was talking about. I had to kick my acting skills into high gear.

"What's wrong with everyone?" I asked innocently.

"This is all your fault!" She was still screaming and the remaining women were looking at me intently.

That's when Oliver came running in. He took just a moment to take in the scene and gave me the oddest look.

"How is this my fault?" I asked her.

"You are the one serving the food and drinks. Something here obviously made everyone sick." Then she started to heave and sprinted to the bathroom.

Thank goodness there were a lot of bathrooms in

that house. I hadn't thought ahead about who would be in charge of the cleanup if people didn't make it. Luckily, they all did.

Then Oliver turned to me. "How did this happen?"

I gave him an innocent look. "How should I know? I didn't cook any of the food, you did." It was wrong to betray him like that, but I really had no choice. I obviously didn't think the whole thing through.

"What the hell happened here?" We both turned around to see Adam walking up behind us.

"We don't know." Oliver responded, shrugging his shoulders and glaring at me. "Everyone just got sick."

"Maybe we should call an ambulance," he said, looking around. "Or several. There are a lot of sick people here. They may have food poisoning."

"No, it's not food poisoning." Sarah said, carefully walking back into the room. She was still holding her stomach and now was holding up a small bottle.

Oh no. I knew I was about to get into really big trouble.

"Let's get everyone out of here and on their way home. Then we can talk." She told us as she started herding the nauseated women out the door, explaining that they were not poisoned. It was just an innocent mistake. They would feel better by the end of the day. None of them were happy about it, but relieved that it wasn't something more serious.

Several minutes later, once everyone was gone, Sarah gathered us all back together. "Someone," looking directly at me, "gave them Ipecac. It induces vomiting, but is not poisonous." She held up the bottle like a trophy she had just won.

Everyone then turned to look at me. I couldn't believe that I was stupid enough to leave the bottle sitting on the counter in the kitchen. There was no way out of this mess. No one would believe for a second that Oliver had anything to do with this. It was me and they all knew it.

I looked down at my feet in shame.

"Why would you do this?" Adam asked me.

Time to come clean. "Because the women were all making fun of me, telling me how stupid I was for getting pregnant, and laughing about it."

Then Adam realized that Oliver was standing there and he didn't want him to know about the stuff we all had cooking.

"Thank you for your help, Oliver. You can go back to work now," Adam said dismissively.

It was quite obvious that Oliver wanted badly to stay and hear what was going on, but he turned and left. The gossip mill would already have enough to keep them busy after today. We didn't need to add anymore fuel to that fire.

"Really, what were you thinking?" Sarah said softly. She was clearly still feeling sick. I thought she might take off any second for the bathroom.

"I'm sorry. It was stupid. I promise not to do anything like that ever again."

"Just please go finish helping Oliver clean up," she said, waving her hand dismissively at me. "And, please don't tell him what this was all about."

They very badly wanted to yell at me. I could see it in their faces. But, they held back. My guess was that they were afraid that if they came down on me too hard that I would just leave, taking the baby with me. I could see the fear in their faces. As long as I was carrying this baby, I was in charge. They knew that, and I knew that. Even so, I had a feeling that this was not going to blow over anytime soon.

CHAPTER 22

Remember a while back when I was telling you about the really bad storm I was driving in? Well, here's the rest of that story.

It had been about a year since I first got into trouble and ran away from home and came to live at the Tyler ranch. One night a really bad storm was headed our way. That's all the TV news had been talking about for a couple of days. It wasn't going to be so bad that we needed to evacuate to a safer area, but bad enough that everyone was strongly encouraged to stay indoors and ride it out.

I needed to talk to Sarah about dinner preparations, so I went to look for her. I found Sarah and Violet together in the dining room talking. Adam was out of town on business, so it was pretty much just the three of us in the house, plus a couple of the staff. When I walked into the room, it went silent. They were certainly acting strange.

"Hi. I just came in to find out what you would like for dinner?" I looked between the two of them.

"Abigail, what exactly do you plan to do once this baby is born?" Violet looked at my stomach when she said that.

"I...I..plan to get another job somewhere and move out." I wasn't prepared for the question and stuttered over my answer.

"That's good, because Sarah and Adam certainly don't need you hanging around confusing things."

"I wasn't planning to hang around. Didn't we already talk about this?" I asked, a bit sarcastically.

"I'm just making sure that we are all still on track. I didn't make all of this happen for nothing, you know," Violet blurted out.

"What? You didn't make anything happen," I said back to her.

That woman was so frustrating. She had to make sure to take credit even when there was no credit due to her.

Sarah looked at both of us with anger written all over her face. Even though she was mostly civil, it was going to be a while until she forgave any of us.

Violet saw the look Sarah gave us. "Oh come now, Sarah. You didn't really think that Abigail cooked this all up on her own, did you? We planned it from the beginning."

"Yes, I'm painfully aware of that." Sarah tensed her jaw when she said that.

"No we didn't! She came to me and told me she wanted me to seduce Adam and get pregnant, and I told her no!"

"Yet, that's exactly what happened, isn't it?" Violet said smugly, looking directly at me.

"Well..yes. I guess. But, not because you wanted me to." I didn't sound convincing at all.

"I don't believe this. Both of you are pathetic!" Sarah screamed at us and stormed out of the room.

Who could blame her? As much as I didn't like Sarah, she was clearly the victim in all of it. Adam cheated on her. I betrayed her by sleeping with her husband. Violet instigated the whole thing. Sarah didn't do anything wrong. I kind of felt sorry for her. She certainly had the right to blow up at us now and then. I would have to find her later and apologize once again.

I glared at Violet. "What the hell? Was that really necessary? You got what you wanted. Why do you feel the need to always make everyone around you miserable!" I ran out and to my room to sulk.

Violet was such a horrible person. Everything was already a mess. I don't know why in the world she felt that she needed to make it worse. It was already difficult to live in that house, with those people, especially considering the crazy situation we were all in. And Violet just had to make sure that everyone knew she was responsible. Like she was going to win some sort of prize or something. Well, maybe she was. She probably thought of my child as her prize in all of this. She manipulated all of us and in the end will get exactly what she wanted. A grandchild. My child. And I was just stupid enough to play my part in her twisted game. She was manipulating all of our lives, and we just let it happen.

She really wasn't though, no matter what she thought. It was all just a stupid mistake on my part. Or was it? Did I subconsciously make all of this happen? I would have to think about that one. Either way, I thought that Violet was making a huge mistake. Now Sarah was furious at her. That was not going to make things any easier around the estate.

A little while later I realized that I never found out from Sarah what to prepare for dinner. So, I cleaned myself up and went looking for her again. I was just about to walk into the library when I heard two people talking. Arguing actually. The door was shut and with the wind howling outside, I was having a hard time hearing. I heard Violet's voice, but couldn't tell who the other person was. Even though I could tell that they were arguing, they were trying to keep their voices low. I stuck my ear to the door, but it didn't help. It was probably Sarah in there. Who else? I'm sure it would take a really long time before Sarah forgave Violet for all she had done. Sarah was probably giving her a piece of her mind. I really wished I could hear what they were saying, since it was probably about me.

Not long before my altercation earlier with Violet and Sarah, I saw Violet in the parlor drinking her 'tea.' So, I was pretty sure she was sloshed by that point. It was her nightly ritual. I really couldn't tell through the door though. I did hear my name. Why was it that whenever someone was having an argument in that house, my name always came up? I tried to listen for a couple more minutes, but really couldn't make anything out, so I started heading toward my room.

I saw Sarah walking toward me in the hall, heading for the library probably, and she stopped to speak to me. I knew then that it wasn't her in there arguing with Violet. That surprised me. Who in the world was in there then?

"Abbey, please make liver and onions for dinner. Since Adam is out of town, it's the perfect time, because he hates them. I know it's one of Violet's favorite meals. Though right now I don't care if she is all that happy or not." She paused for a moment, thinking about Violet I'm sure. "Well, anyway, go ahead and make that tonight."

"Okay sure," I told her. "Oliver just picked some up at the store yesterday. I'm heading that way, I'll go tell him right now."

"All right. I'll let Violet know," she said. "I think she's in the library."

"She is," I replied as I continued on down the hall toward the kitchen.

A few seconds later I heard Sarah scream and I turned around and started running toward the sound. The library door was open then, and I ran in. What I found made me turn white. It was Violet, laying face up on the floor in a pool of her own blood. There was a knife on the floor beside her. Sarah was just standing there staring at her, doing nothing. I knelt on the floor to check on Violet. She was still alive and bleeding profusely from several stab wounds. She was wearing a white blouse and there was a lot of blood. The entire thing was a deep crimson color. I looked up at Sarah, who looked like she was going to faint.

"It wasn't me, I swear!" Sarah blurted out, raising up her hands to show me that there was no blood on her.

I looked around and saw that the back door to the library was wide open. The wind was howling right outside and making its way in. Sarah had only been in the room for under ten seconds when I heard her scream and went running back to the library. So, it was very obvious that she couldn't have stabbed Violet several times, opened the back door, and screamed to get my attention in that short of time. Besides, when I arrived a few seconds later, Violet was already bleeding quite a bit and was unconscious. It looked as if she had been lying there for a few minutes. She was probably stabbed right after I walked away from the library and while I stood in the hall talking to Sarah. It is surprising that we didn't hear a struggle or any screaming from Violet.

"I believe you," I told her. "You're the doctor, do something!" I yelled at her.

She was already scanning the room for something. She walked over and picked up a small blanket and then knelt down to put pressure on the wounds.

"Call 911," she ordered.

I was already reaching for the phone on the desk. The operator on the other end told me that due to the storm, their emergency personnel were all out on calls and it would be at least an hour before they could get there. From what I could see, Violet didn't have that long. I hung up the phone and turned to Sarah.

"They can't get here for at least an hour. Can you help her?" I started shaking then. I didn't know if it was from the trauma of the bloody scene in front of me or from the freezing storm coming in through the still wide open back door.

"No. She needs surgery. There's nothing I can do here. I'm not a surgeon. She is going to bleed out and die if we don't get her to a hospital right away."

I could see Sarah shaking like a leaf. She was a doctor, or at least almost, I think. Why would she be so freaked out?

"Are you okay?" I asked her as I jumped up and ran over to shut the back door.

"Yes. I know I should be more calm. I have seen this type of thing before when I worked at the hospital, but when it's your own family, it's different. Please, I need you to drive us to the hospital." She sounded so desperate.

"Me? I don't know how to drive very well. I've only had a couple of lessons and don't have a license." Adam had given me some driving lessons, certainly not enough to know how to maneuver a car through a storm and get there quickly before someone died. The thought completely unnerved me.

"It will have to do. I can't drive right now. I'm too upset. I don't really know how to drive anyway. We have a driver. I never needed to learn." She told me. "Since Adam isn't here, it's up to us to try to save her. Go get the car!"

It was not the time to argue about who was the worst driver, so I jumped up and ran as fast as I could outside. It only took me a minute or so to get back with the car. I parked it right in front of the door. One of the housekeepers helped us carry Violet to the car. She was the only person in the house we could find. I told her to call Adam and let him know what was going on and to meet us at the hospital as soon as he could. Then we headed out into the night.

CHAPTER 23

I drove in the storm for quite a while, still not knowing if Violet would live or die. It was one of the most terrifying things I have ever done. The storm was not letting up and I barely knew how to drive. Not a great combination. But I was determined to get through it, to fight the forces of nature, and to win. Nothing else on earth mattered at that moment. Violet was conscious off and on, moaning mostly from the backseat. Sarah was doing her best to keep an eye on her. The bleeding had mostly stopped, but Violet was dangerously weak.

When we reached the narrow bridge that crossed over the river, I could see that the water was very high and raging wildly. It was actually overflowing the banks and threatening the bridge itself. I don't know how this was even possible. How long had it been raining? Certainly not long enough for this to happen. But, there it was, right in front of me, very close and threatening.

While crossing the bridge, it suddenly felt like we hit a patch of ice, which was impossible, because it was a summer storm. But that's what it felt like. I had the steering wheel in a death grip. The car started skidding and there was not much I could do about it. I took my foot off the gas and turned into the skid, knowing that was what I was supposed to do, but it wasn't helping. The car seemed to have a mind of its own. I could see, and feel, the bridge railing coming straight for us. For a moment I wasn't sure if we were skidding toward the railing or if it had broken loose and was flying toward us. It felt like it was all happening in slow motion.

Then the unthinkable happened. We hit the railing, it gave way, and the car with all of us in it, flew over the edge and straight into the water. Luckily, we didn't fall far because the water was almost overflowing the bridge. The car went in, nose first and my head slammed into the steering wheel, knocking me unconscious. That's when everything became so serene, like I was floating away. I didn't want to wake up. It was weird because I was definitely out, but sort of aware of what was going on. Kind of like a dream. It didn't last long though. Very quickly I started feeling the layers of darkness, the blackness peeling away, bit by bit. As I was coming out of the serenity, I could feel someone tugging at me. I instinctively swatted at them.

"Stop it!" I heard Sarah yell at me.

"What..what are you doing?" I still wasn't fully awake. "Ow, that's my leg!"

"I know," she yelled back. "It's stuck under the dashboard. We have to get it out. This is going to hurt."

That's when I realized where we were and what was happening. I started crying. "What about the baby?" I looked down and put my hand on my stomach. It was very still, which scared me more than anything else happening at that moment.

"I don't know. Let's get you out and then we can check on the baby," she said, yanking on my leg again.

"Ouch! That hurts!"

With that last jerk, my leg came free. My jeans were ripped and I could see that my leg was gashed pretty bad and bleeding. It didn't matter though. The car was filling up with water fast and we needed to get out of there. The water was freezing and we were both shivering terribly. If we didn't drown, we were going to all die of hypothermia.

"We need to get out of here!" Sarah yelled above the storm.

"What about Violet?" She was unconscious in the backseat.

"We can't help her if we both drown. Let's get you out first, then I'll come back for her."

"You can't leave her here. You won't get back in time to save her." I yelled back. The car was slowly starting to float down the river, and was picking up speed. Sarah would never be able to get back to it.

"Stop arguing with me. I can't carry both of you. You are the one that is pregnant and I'm getting you out first!" Sarah meant it too.

I had no choice but to agree. I was bleeding badly and needed Sarah's help to get out. We were wasting time by arguing about it, and needed to do something immediately, or all of us would drown. So, with the help of Sarah, I squeezed out through the open passenger window. Sarah had had enough sense about her to roll her window down the second we hit the water. I was a pretty good swimmer, but Sarah still had to help me. With only one good leg, and a very large belly, swimming was almost impossible in the fast flowing river. Luckily it was not a very wide river and we made it to the bank in just a few minutes. I pulled myself up on the bank far enough so that I was out of the river completely. Sarah sat down next to me to catch her breath.

"You need to go back for Violet," I told her. With my injured leg, I was of no use.

"Look." Sarah pointed toward the river.

I turned and saw the car floating away. I tried to stand up. We had to go after the car. Sarah grabbed my arm and pulled me back down.

"What are you doing? You can't go in there." She held onto me tightly.

"I have to try. We can't let her drown," I replied. I tried to pull free of her, but she wasn't about to let me go.

"You are hurt and pregnant. You wouldn't be able to get to the car if you tried anyway. I won't let you go. It's too late, Abbey."

She was right. The river was moving fast and the car was too far by then to go after it. It was too late. There was nothing we could do. Even if I thought I had a chance to get to the car, it would just be stupid. I couldn't, I wouldn't, put my baby at risk.

"Oh my god," was all I could say.

I didn't even like Violet, yet I burst out crying. I wasn't even sure why. I guess I just felt so useless. I didn't know how in the world we were going to tell Adam.

"Hey, this is not your fault. It just happened. Someone else stabbed her. We were trying to save her.

I don't think there is anything else we could have done." She was trying to make me feel better, but it really didn't help.

"Besides," she continued, "I didn't want to get into it in the car while I was trying to get you out, but Violet was already dead when we hit the water."

"What? Are you sure?" I was very surprised.

"I'm sure. I checked her pulse while you were unconscious. So see, she died from the stab wounds. There was nothing we could have done."

Even though Violet had died, and that was horrible, I actually felt a bit better, knowing that none of this was because I drove us over a bridge. Still, I felt really bad. I knew that Adam would be devastated. Violet certainly had her faults, she was horrible to me, but she was his mother and he loved her dearly.

For a few minutes Sarah and I just sat there, holding each other and crying, in the pouring rain. It really wasn't Violet we were crying for, it was Adam. Regardless of our feelings for each other, we both loved Adam and couldn't even fathom how much this was going to hurt him.

Someone must have seen the accident, because right about then, two police cars and an ambulance pulled up along side us on the bank of the river. There was a road right behind us that followed along the river. We weren't even aware of its existence until the emergency vehicles showed up. They brought a gurney and put me in the ambulance first. Sarah was fine, other than a bit of hypothermia. They gave her a warming blanket and she crawled in the ambulance to ride to the hospital with me. One of the police officers told us that he would meet us at the hospital. Sarah held my hand the entire way. It was such a loving gesture. I wondered if we could be friends.

When we arrived, the emergency staff took me in right away to tend to my leg. Luckily I didn't need surgery. It was not as bad as I originally thought, and they were able to stitch me up. It hurt worse than it was. They also checked the baby and everything was fine. Just as we were right in the middle of the ultrasound, Adam walked in.

"Do you want to know the sex of the baby?" the doctor asked me.

I looked over at Adam and Sarah. I definitely wanted to know, but I would leave it up to them. They both nodded expectantly.

"Yes," I told the doctor.

"Okay then. You are having a girl and everything seems to be coming along nicely. Your little swim in the river doesn't seem to have bothered her at all. She's definitely a tough one."

We all smiled. A baby girl. Wow. All of a sudden the whole thing sank in. I was having a baby. This was actually happening. I burst out crying, which I seemed to do a lot lately. The doctor looked at me with a furrowed brow.

"Are you all right?" he asked.

"Yes. I'm fine," I said between sobs. "I was just so scared."

He looked up at Adam and Sarah and they said they

would stay with me. He told them that I was just fine and to keep me off the leg for a few days. I could go home in the morning. Then he left.

"Why are you crying?" Adam asked me.

"This all just seems so much more real all of a sudden," I told him, between sniffles.

"I know what you mean," he said. "Oh, what room is my mother in?"

I stopped crying immediately. While dealing with my injured leg and worrying about the baby, I had almost forgotten about Violet. Sarah and I looked at each other.

"What?" Adam said, looking back and forth between us.

"Um, let's go out in the hallway." Sarah took his hand and they walked out of the room.

I was really glad that she did that. I was certainly not strong enough to tell him. She could do it. She was his wife after all. I could see them through the window. They were standing right outside my room. She talked for about 30 seconds, then he hugged her and started sobbing. It was one of the most heart wrenching scenes I had ever witnessed. I turned my head to stare at the opposite wall, because all of a sudden, I felt like I was eavesdropping on a very private moment. That was when I realized that he would never be mine. He belonged to Sarah, and always would.

I turned back a few minutes later, and they were gone. I was relieved and closed my eyes to rest. I must have fallen asleep, because the next thing I knew, daylight was streaming in through the hospital room window. I heard snoring and looked over to see Adam fast asleep in a chair in my room. I started to get up to go to the bathroom and he jumped up.

"What are you doing?" He asked me, coming over to stand by the side of the bed. "You should stay in bed."

"I have to pee."

"Hold on, let me get the nurse to help you." He quickly left the room.

The nurse came in and helped me get to the bathroom and get dressed. They were processing the paperwork and I would get to go home soon. Adam waited with me.

"Are you okay?" I asked him, while we waited.

"Yeah, I guess. Sarah told me everything that happened last night. I want to thank you for trying to save my mother. I know that must have been very scary for you."

"You don't have to thank me. But, you're welcome. I'm just sorry that we couldn't get her to the hospital in time."

"Are you the one that stabbed her?" He asked very calmly.

Oh boy, his gratitude certainly didn't last long.

"What? No. Why would you ask me that?" I was shocked at the question.

"Because Sarah said she saw you walking away from the library just as she went in and found my mother laying on the floor."

"So Sarah is accusing me of stabbing her? You

have got to be kidding." I was starting to get angry. How could she do that to me after all that we had just been through together?

"The truth is that I had been listening at the door. Your mother was arguing with someone, I don't know who. Since I felt I should just stay out of it, I left. That's when Sarah stopped me and we talked for a couple of minutes. Did she also tell you that the back door to the library was wide open when she went in? Someone obviously took off right after the fight."

Adam sat there quietly, contemplating everything I had just said.

"No, she didn't tell me that part."

"That's what I figured. Maybe you should get the whole story before you come in here accusing me of killing your mother." He already hated me, so I didn't think anything I said at that point was going to make it worse.

CHAPTER 24

Two days later they found the car with Violet still in it. That's how long it took for the storm to clear up and the water to recede enough for them to find it. It had floated several miles down the river and was found wedged in a pile of large boulders next to the bank. A couple of pre-teen boys came across it as they were walking along the river road above.

Because of the stab wounds, an autopsy was done. The results shocked everyone.

We were all standing in the living room when the call came in. I wasn't invited, of course, but I heard Sarah and Adam talking as I walked down the hall. Then the phone rang and I walked in. I was definitely part of everything that happened, which is probably why no one said anything about my being there with them. We were all waiting on news about Violet, and the entire house had been tense for the past two days. Without even asking, I could tell that Adam was talking to someone official. I don't know exactly who though. It didn't really matter. Sarah and I sat quietly and waited for the news.

When Adam hung up the phone, his face looked like it had been drained of all the blood. He had gone white and couldn't even speak. It took a moment for him to collect himself. He looked as if he were trying very hard not to cry. Sarah and I stood up and waited for him to talk to us. Finally he composed himself.

He explained that the coroner found that Violet did not die from her stab wounds, as we all (well most of us) thought. She drowned. What that boiled down to was that Sarah lied. Violet was not already dead when the car went over the bridge. Sarah left her there to drown. She was probably hoping that Violet's body would never be found. No such luck. I was absolutely horrified that she would do something like that.

"I can't believe that you just let my mother drown!" Adam yelled.

I looked over at Sarah as he said this. I had no idea how in the world she was going to explain her actions.

"Abbey! Don't you have anything to say for yourself?" he asked me.

"What? Me?" I pointed at myself as I looked from Adam to Sarah and back. "Wait, I thought you were talking to Sarah." I was thoroughly confused.

"Why would I be talking to Sarah?" He said with a growing attitude in his voice.

"Because she is the one that left your mother, alive, in the car to float away and drown. I was injured, up on the bank of the river. And pregnant. Don't forget that part. I tried to get her to go back to get Violet and she refused."

"You are lying!" Sarah screamed.

"You know I'm not lying." I was trying to be calm. "I begged you to go in after her and you said she was already dead. You could have gone back in and saved her."

"Why are you saying that?" Sarah said directly to me. Then she turned to her husband.

"Adam, after I helped her to the river bank, I

wanted to go back for your mother. I didn't tell you this before because I didn't want to hurt you anymore than you were already hurting, but Abbey grabbed onto me and wouldn't let me go. Your mother was still in the car, screaming. It was horrible, but I couldn't pull away from Abbey quick enough to get to her. That's the truth. I swear." Sarah told him all of that with a dead serious look on her face and even managed to squeeze out a tiny teardrop, for emphasis. The woman deserved an Oscar for her performance. I almost believed her and I knew it was all a lie.

Adam glared at me.

"Oh my god. You don't believe her, do you?" I asked him. He couldn't possibly believe such a wild, ridiculous story.

I had a bad feeling that this was not going to go my way.

"There's no reason for Sarah to lie. I believe her." Adam said, taking her hand.

"Are you kidding me?" I was shocked. "She had every reason. She hated your mother. Violet was horrible to her. And to me. You are the only one that she was nice to. Of course she never treated us poorly when you were around. But, she was a holy terror when you were out of town. I guarantee you that Sarah hated her, every bit as much as I did." I laid it all out for them.

"Really?" Adam asked. "You just admitted that you hated my mother. That sounds a lot like motive to me. I'm calling the cops." He made a move for the phone.

I saw Sarah smile and I gave her a look that caused

her to immediately lose the stupid grin on her face. Then I lunged for the phone and got to it just as Adam did. He was surprised by how quick I was.

"What are you doing?" He asked as he yanked the receiver from my hand.

"Adam, please don't call the cops. Do you really want to put the mother of your child in jail?" I knew Sarah would hate that I called myself that.

"You are not the mother of his child. I am." Sarah chimed in.

"Is that right? Well, we'll see about that!" And I stormed out of the room without another word. They never did call the police on me.

****

A few days later, the police called Adam back. They told him that even though Violet ultimately drowned, they were treating it as a murder. She was stabbed after all. Adam and Sarah seemed to have forgotten that part. They had been so focused on the fact that I drove over the bridge and left her to drown. I knew the truth though. So did Sarah, whether she wanted to admit it or not.

Now that everyone was focusing on Violet being stabbed, the accusations started flying. I was not immune. However, I knew I was innocent and did my best to ignore them. I was sure that Sarah knew I didn't do it. She saw me in the hallway right before she walked into the library and found Violet stabbed. I was calm and had no blood on me. I was certainly not someone that could have a fight and stab someone, then calmly walk down the hall like nothing had happened. It would have been written all over my face and those things would have been obvious to anyone walking by.

Because Adam was the sole heir to his parents' estate, he got it all. This was no surprise to anyone. I was sort of hoping that Violet would leave me, or at least my baby, some money. Especially since my child would be her only grandchild, and she did promise me a lot of money if I got pregnant. But that didn't happen. It was probably my fault that she didn't leave me anything. I should have just told her that I did get pregnant on purpose. At least she might have honored her end of the deal then. But it was Violet. Who knew what was in that crazy old lady's head. She may never have had any intention of coming through with her promise. Once I got pregnant, there was no way to force her to pay anything. She knew that. At least this way I could honestly say that I did not get pregnant on purpose, just to make Violet happy, and to make some money. I would hate to have to explain that to my daughter one day.

CHAPTER 25

Could I really give up my baby to those horrid people? Would that make me the worst mother ever? Yes, it might. I had to talk to Adam about it. Just him and me. Sarah was not invited. I didn't need her spewing anymore of her lies. I found Adam working in the library and walked in quietly, determined to get the truth out once and for all.

"Adam, can we talk?"

He didn't even look up from his desk. I just stood there for another minute waiting.

"Adam?"

"What do we have to talk about?" he finally responded, still not looking up at me.

"The baby." I walked over and sat down in a chair across from his desk.

"What about it?"

"Her," I said.

"What? Oh, yeah. Her. What about her? I thought all of this was settled," he answered.

He seemed really preoccupied with whatever he was reading on his desk. Kind of half paying attention to anything I said.

"Not really."

"What do you mean?" he asked, finally focusing those green eyes right into mine. I had his attention then.

"I mean, I'm having second thoughts about all of this. I don't know if I can give up my baby."

I knew it wasn't fair of me to change my mind, yet again. But I couldn't help it. She was my baby and I had had a lot of time to think about what I was doing. Since Violet wasn't around to stick her nose in the middle of it all and confuse me with all of her nonsense, I was having a very hard time sticking to my end of the bargain. Handing my baby over to Sarah would tear me apart.

Adam started turning red and looked really angry. Then I saw him take a deep breath and wait a minute before replying to me. He looked to me as though he was trying very hard not to say something he might regret later.

"Abbey, we made a deal," he said calmly, letting out his breath slowly.

"I know. But I love her." I looked down and rubbed my ever increasing belly.

"Of course you do. But, you are so young. What kind of life can you give her? You can't even afford to take care of yourself. How could you rent a decent place to live, not to mention being able to buy formula, diapers, clothes, and a million other things that babies need?"

"Well, I thought that's where you would come in. She is your daughter after all," I answered back.

"No." That was all he said.

"What do you mean by that? You aren't going to help support your own child? You are just going to let us live on the streets, with no money for food?" I started getting angry. "You couldn't possibly do that to your own daughter, could you?" I probably sounded desperate, but that's exactly how I felt.

"That's not what I mean at all. I mean that no, I won't give you money for any of that. My daughter is staying right here with me. You can fight me on this, but I have the means to fight you all the way in court. You will never win. Is that what you want, to have a big legal battle with me?" He wasn't backing down.

"No. But, you can't stop me from leaving here and then you'll never find me. Never find us," I threatened.

"Really? Well let me tell you a little secret." He smiled. "Ever since you told us that you were pregnant, we've had someone watching you day and night. There is literally nowhere that you can hide. I will always know where you are." He was still grinning. It was a bit creepy.

"How can you do this?" I asked. "You said you loved me."

"Loved. As in the past tense. I thought I loved you once, yes. That is no longer the case. I love Sarah and we are going to raise this baby together. Without you." He was dead serious and a bit scary. "And, if you cause me any trouble, I will make sure that you go to prison for killing my mother. I still don't know for sure if it was you or not, but I'll do it anyway, just so I can have that baby. So, don't you dare even consider trying to leave this house. You will be staying here until my daughter is born and let everyone think Sarah is the mother. Do I make myself clear?"

He succeeded in scaring me. I nodded my head, got up and walked out of the room, slamming the door behind me. I burst out crying before I was even ten feet out the door. I doubt Adam heard me as I ran the rest of the way to my room. I laid on my bed for hours trying to figure a way out of the huge mess I was in. He was right, I had no money to fight him for custody and I had no money to leave and support myself and a baby. What was I thinking? Maybe I could go back and live with my parents? No, that wouldn't work. I couldn't bear to face them. After all that I had put them through, how could I possibly show up on their doorstep with a child? Besides, if Adam really did have eyes on me, he could still get the baby no matter where I was. I started looking around my room, expecting to see someone hiding in the closet watching me. I was being ridiculous. No one was in the room with me. But, I really wouldn't have been surprised to find someone in the hallway keeping an eye on my door.

Suddenly there was a knock on my bedroom door. That was very strange, since no one ever came to my room. I didn't answer because I was in no mood to have a fight with anyone.

"Abbey, it's Sarah. Can I come in?" I heard though the door.

Still I said nothing. I didn't want to deal with her. Maybe if I ignored her, she would go away.

"Abbey, please. Can we talk?" This time she didn't wait for an answer and just walked in.

"Not now Sarah." I was still lying on the bed, and I rolled away so my back was facing her. If that didn't get my point across, nothing would.

"I just want to see how you are doing. Adam told

me about your talk." She sat down on the bed next to me.

"You mean our fight," I responded without moving.

"He said you had a talk about the baby and you were upset when you left."

That made me turn around and sit up to face her. "Is that what he told you? That we talked and I was upset? Well, he was right about me being upset. But there was no talk. He demanded that I let you continue pretending to be pregnant and threatened to have me imprisoned if I left with my baby. Is that what you meant by having a talk?" I made sure there was plenty of sarcasm in my voice.

"Oh. Well, I'm sorry. That's not what he told me."

"Yeah, right. I don't believe you. The two of you are constantly working on ways to get me to give you this baby and get out of your lives. I'm not an idiot." I didn't have anything to lose, so, I had no problem telling her what was on my mind.

"Look, I don't think you're an idiot. We are not working together on this. Well, not on all of what you just told me anyway. I just want a baby and you promised me that. I had no idea Adam was threatening you. I don't want it to be like that. This needs to be your choice. We can't and won't force anything on you."

"The two of you need to get your stories straight. It seems like every time I have a conversation with one of you, it is completely the opposite of what the other said."

"I don't know about that," Sarah responded.

"Why are you all of a sudden being so nice to me? You've been nothing but nasty from the moment I walked in the door, especially after you found out about the affair. You think being nice to me now is going to get you your way?"

"I don't want to fight with you about this. I'm going to go talk to Adam. Let's take tonight for everyone to calm down and we can talk later. Please don't go anywhere until we figure this all out. Okay?" She seemed sincere and stood up to leave.

"How am I going to go anywhere when Adam has someone spying on me 24 hours a day?"

She actually looked confused when I said that. Somehow I was sure that she had no idea that he was spying on me.

Since I couldn't get a straight answer out of anyone, I decided to follow Sarah and find out exactly what was going on. She went directly to their bedroom, and I followed, keeping a safe distance away. She had no idea I was behind her. She was a woman on a mission. When the door slammed behind her, I stuck my ear to it. Eavesdropping was starting to become a way of life for me.

"Did you threaten to have Abbey arrested if she didn't give us the baby?"

"Who told you that?" he asked sheepishly. He knew perfectly well who told her.

"She did. Arrested for what?"

"For killing my mother. What else could it be? You

need to stop talking to her. She is twisting everything up." He sounded angry.

"That's pretty much what she said to me. Abbey said that we need to get our stories straight. She's got a point. We don't seem to know what each other is doing, or saying." She was definitely upset with him. "You need to stop threatening her. That is only going to make it worse. If she thinks she is going to get arrested for Violet's murder, then she is going to run, and there won't be much we can do about it. And, did you tell Abbey that we have someone watching her around the clock?"

"Yes. I do. I can't take any chance that she will run off in the middle of the night, taking my daughter with her."

"Your daughter? I thought she was our daughter." Sarah sounded a bit hurt by that.

"You know what I mean," he replied. "Yes, of course she is our daughter. We will be raising her together. We just need to keep Abbey calm until after she gives birth."

"Well threatening her with imprisonment is not the way to do that," Sarah told him.

"I guess you are right. I'll tone it down," Adam relented. "But I won't let up on the surveillance. We need to keep an eye on her."

I figured that was the end of the argument and decided to get away to think about things before I got caught. I went upstairs to our private room on the third floor and locked myself in. I just wanted to be alone. It was unlikely that anyone would find me in there, except Adam, maybe. But, I doubted he would even be looking for me.

The second I walked in, I noticed it. The painting. The Picasso to be exact, was gone. What in the world? Where could it have gone? I think Adam and I were the only ones that even knew about the Picasso. He did have one of the staff clean the room occasionally, but I'm sure she had no idea of the painting's worth. He made it a point not to talk about it to anyone. He said it made him feel vulnerable that such a priceless thing was in his home. If people knew about it, we could all be in danger.

I searched the room to see if someone just took it off the wall for some reason. It was not in the closet, or anywhere else, that I could find. I started to shiver, not from the cold, but probably from nervousness or fright. Would that cause goosebumps? Anyway, I turned and ran to find Adam.

Obviously his fight with Sarah was over, because I found Adam out in the stables talking to Walter. I smiled and gave Walter a hug when I saw him. He had been my confidant through my ordeal at the ranch and was almost like a father to me. He knew all about the pregnancy, and who the father was, and never judged me. Adam gave me a weird look when I hugged Walter, but didn't say anything.

"Adam, can I talk to you?" I asked, and Walter just walked away without saying a word.

"What is it?"

"I was just up in the third floor room and the Picasso is gone!" Then I realized I was a bit too loud.

Looking around, I lowered my voice. "The Picasso is missing," I said much more quietly.

"What? What are you talking about? Where is it?" He sounded surprised.

"I have no idea. That's why I'm here talking to you. I thought maybe you put it somewhere else, or sold it or something."

"What did you do with it?" he asked me.

"Me? I didn't do anything with it. It was gone when I got there." I could not believe he was actually accusing me of taking it.

"Well it was there the last time I was in that room. You are the only one that knows about it. There's no one else." He glared at me.

"There obviously is someone else. Don't you dare accuse me of taking it. I'm not a thief!" I screamed, and I didn't care who heard me that time. I was furious that he thought I took it. What in the world would I do with it if I did take it? I didn't have the slightest idea where to sell a painting like that.

"Keep your voice down," he said, while patting the air to accentuate his seriousness, I guess.

"If I took that stupid painting, why would I still be living and working here? I would be able to sell it for enough money to live the rest of my life on." I really hoped that I was convincing. He didn't need to know that I didn't have a clue what to do with the painting.

"Maybe to keep the heat off of you," he replied.

"Oh my god, you have lost your damn mind. I'm done with this conversation," I told him and walked out.

CHAPTER 26

I ran straight to Walter and asked for a ride into town. Walter obliged without even asking where we were going or why. I spent several minutes in his truck complaining about Adam. Walter did a lot of head nodding and said 'yep' a lot. He was not a stupid man. He knew better than to get into a conversation that was all about the boss. I knew that. But it was nice to have someone that would just sit and listen to me. I never felt judged. I can honestly say that, other than Huck, Walter was the only person in that whole town that treated me with any kindness. I loved our long talks. I told him some about my past, without revealing too much about what a loser I used to be. He knew I was now pregnant with Adam's child. He tried to give me advice here and there. But, he really just let me do the talking for the most part, and that was fine with me. I would like to think that if my daughter did end up being raised on the ranch, that Walter would be there for her. I knew I could trust him with her life.

As soon as we reached Huck's house, I thanked Walter and got out of the truck. I told him he didn't have to wait for me, but he said he was not going to leave me until he knew I was safe in the house. They certainly didn't make 'em like that anymore.

When I knocked on the door, a beautiful blonde woman answered. I immediately realized that I had never been to his house before. He once pointed it out to me, but we didn't go in that time. I also realized that I had never met anyone in his family. I guess I had been so caught up in my own little world, that I didn't get out much. That sounded really selfish and would have to change.

"Hello, can I help you?" she asked me.

"Um, hi. Is Huck home?" I asked nervously.

"Yes, come on in." She took a good look at my belly as I walked in and her eyes got wide. At that moment I could tell exactly what she was thinking.

"Uh, my boyfriend and I are expecting a baby girl. Huck and I are just friends," I blurted out.

With a look of relief on her face, she said "I see. You are awful young, aren't you?"

"Mom. Be nice."

We both turned to see Huck walking in from the back part of the house. He smiled at me. Those green eyes, just gorgeous. I looked at his mother then. He was right, they had the same beautiful green eyes.

"I was being nice. Wasn't I?" She turned to me.

"Yes, of course. We were just talking, Huck. It's fine," I told him.

"Well, I have some things to do. It was nice meeting you...oh, I just realized I didn't get your name." She looked at me, waiting for an answer.

"Abbey."

"It's nice to meet you. There's some cookies and stuff in the kitchen if you two kids would like a snack." Then we were alone.

"What are you doing here?" he asked. "You've never come here before."

"I know. I just wanted to talk to you." I started

walking around the room, looking at the family photos. "You have a nice family," I said, picking up one of the photos that was sitting on the fireplace mantel. "Is this your sister? She's cute." I held up the photo for him to see.

"Yes. Remember, I told you about her? She died a few years ago. She was only six years old." He looked sad when he said that.

"Oh yeah. That's right. I'm sorry. Her name was Madeline, right?"

"No, Madison. Her name was Madison."

"Oh. That's a pretty name. I like it."

I put the photo down and continued walking around the room, looking at the photos of a happy family. There were pictures of them at the zoo, at Thanksgiving with a large group of people, at the beach, pretty much everywhere that I could see. I was suddenly very jealous of his perfect life. Yes, I had parents, and I knew they loved me, but my father worked all the time, and we really didn't go out and do that much as a family. Besides, I never had a brother or sister to share things with. I know that Huck's sister died, but he was really lucky that he had her in his life, even for such a short time. That's something I would never have.

"Abbey, why are you here? Something's up, isn't it?"

"Adam and I had a fight."

"Another one?" He rolled his eyes. "I don't know why you put up with him. You don't need to deal with him."

"He is the father of my baby. I kind of have to deal with him, whether I like it or not."

"No you don't. You can leave anytime you want. You aren't his prisoner," he proclaimed, like it was the first time I had heard it.

"Really? With what? You know I don't have any money."

"I have a job. I can loan you some money." He seemed so sincere in his offer.

"No. Definitely not. I can't take your money."

"But you can take Adam's?" he asked me.

"It's his baby. So, yes, I can take his money." I didn't feel one bit guilty about taking money from the father of my child. It was his responsibility after all.

He rolled his eyes again.

"I saw that," I smiled.

"Well never mind about that right now. I have something I need to tell you." He looked serious all of a sudden.

"Okay, what?"

"I ran into Teresa yesterday. She was being nice so we hung out for a bit. I didn't see the harm in it. I did really care for her once. The cafe was dead and we just sat there talking."

"I see. So why are you telling me?" I was a bit annoyed. I didn't want Huck as a boyfriend, but Teresa was not the right one for him.

"Because it's important. Just pay attention." He folded his arms across his chest, clearly waiting for me to shut up and listen.

"Okay, sorry." He took my hand and we walked over and sat on the couch to talk.

"I was going to go by your house today after work, but since you are here, I can tell you now. Teresa told me that she was blackmailing Violet."

"Really? About what?" I was definitely getting more curious.

"Just hold on. There's more," he continued. "She said she knows that you are the one that's pregnant with Adam's baby, not Sarah. She knows Sarah is just faking her pregnancy."

"Oh no."

"Well they got into an argument in the library the night of the big storm and after Teresa threatened to tell everyone what she knows, Violet came at her with a knife. She said Violet was drunk and they fought over the knife and Teresa stabbed Violet in self-defense. Then she panicked and ran out the back door. That's her version of the story anyway."

"Oh my god." I was in shock and sat there thinking about the whole thing for a minute. Huck just waited. "Well that does fit with everything. I heard Violet arguing with someone in the library, then she was stabbed and the person left by the back door. Wow. I can't believe she told all of that to you. Isn't she afraid that you will go to the police?" I asked him.

"No, I don't think so. She said she is in love with me."

"Of course she is." I kind of rolled my eyes.

"I saw that," he smirked.

"What are we going to do? We should call the police, right?" I asked.

After hearing what Teresa confessed to Huck, I was pretty sure the part about Teresa fighting with Violet and stabbing her was correct. But, not entirely sure the part about it being self defense. I could see a drunk Violet coming at her though. I didn't really know. The whole thing was just crazy to me. I was certainly glad that we had police to figure all that stuff out. I don't think I could do it. It's so hard to tell who is lying and who isn't. The whole thing just made my head hurt to think about it.

"You know, Adam has been blaming me for killing Violet. He believes the ridiculous lies Sarah has been telling him."

"Maybe we should go have a talk with him." He was beginning to sound angry. "And let him know exactly what Teresa told me. Then he can deal with the police, not us."

Without waiting for me to respond, he stood up, took my hand and pulled me toward the front door.

"Mom!" he yelled to the other room. "We are going out for a while."

"Okay!" she called back. "Have fun. Nice meeting you Abbey!"

"Let's go," he said as he slammed the front door behind us.

I was starting to get worried that it was not going to go well. Of course it wasn't going to go well. Huck was about to confront Adam about the way he'd been treating me. It definitely was not going to go well at all. I tried to stay calm about the whole thing, for my baby's sake. She was all that mattered to me.

When we arrived at the ranch a few minutes later, Huck pulled right up to the front door and jumped out of the car. He didn't even wait for me to get out and he walked right into the house without knocking. I almost had to run to keep up, and in my condition, that wasn't easy.

"Where is he?" Huck asked the first person he saw, a meek woman in her 40s that I rarely came across. She was one of the housekeepers and I don't think she had ever said a word to me. She just pointed toward the library and Huck grabbed my hand again and headed that way.

"We need to talk to you," he blurted out as we stormed into the library.

Adam and Sarah were sitting on the couch talking. Both jumped up when we burst into the room.

"What's going on?" Sarah asked, clearly confused.

"I'll tell you what's going on," he said directly to her.

I knew this was going to get ugly and I parked myself partially behind Huck, almost hoping they wouldn't notice I was there.

"I had an interesting conversation yesterday with Teresa, your horse trainer."

"What are you talking about?" Adam asked him.

Huck went on to tell him exactly what he told me

earlier, the confession that Teresa made to him about killing Violet in self defense.

"Self defense? Really? You are telling me that Teresa had to fend off my elderly mother with a knife? Teresa is half her age and in really great shape. Your story is ridiculous." He started to turn his back on us in a dismissive manner. Adam obviously didn't believe a word that Huck said.

"You can believe me or not, but that's the truth. Teresa told me all of it. Why would she do that if it weren't true?" Huck asked. "And there's more," he added. "If you think for a second that Abbey was the one that left your mother in the car to die, you are an idiot. I believe her when she says that Sarah knew she was still alive and made no effort to go back for her." Huck was talking to Adam, but looking Sarah straight in the eyes when he said it.

Adam turned to look at Sarah and she just denied it, as usual. Perhaps that truth was never going to come out. It will always be my word against hers. And with everything that had happened, no one would believe a pregnant, run away teenage girl over the lady of the estate.

"Why are you always with Abbey?" Adam asked Huck, with suspicion in his eyes. "Is there something going on that I should know about?"

Huck and I looked at each other. That's when I stepped up. I walked around Huck and looked Adam right in the eyes.

"My relationship with Huck is none of your damn business," I said sternly.

I have no idea why I suddenly felt so brave. Maybe because it really was none of his business. He had no right questioning me on any relationship that I had.

"Is that right?" Adam responded, not backing down. "How do I even know this is my baby?" He quickly looked down to my belly and back up again.

That's when Huck gently pushed me aside and hit Adam. He punched him so hard in the face that Adam stumbled backward over the back of the couch and landed on the floor.

As Adam was getting up, Huck said in a menacing voice to him: "If you don't stop threatening Abbey with all of this, I will kill you myself."

That made Adam stop in his tracks and think twice. I do have to say that Huck sounded deadly serious. I was never so proud of him. I knew that he was in love with me, and that was why he was confronting Adam. I did love him, but it wasn't the same. Even after everything, I was still in love with Adam. I knew it was stupid and foolish, but I couldn't help myself. Even though I was in love, I certainly didn't like Adam at all at that moment.

"I'm calling the police," Sarah said, as she reached for the phone.

The police showed up about an hour later. I made myself scarce, which was fine with Adam and Sarah. I didn't want the police to see me there and start inquiring on why an unrelated pregnant teenager was living there. Huck did stay though. He needed to give his statement because Teresa confessed to him directly. No one told the police about Huck hitting Adam, even though a nice black eye was starting to shine through.

After all the statements were given, the police found Teresa out in the stables and questioned her. I couldn't believe that she was still on the ranch working after all that had happened. She obviously had no idea that Huck would repeat her story to anyone.

The police believed Teresa's story about it being self defense. The autopsy did show that Violet was intoxicated, so that part fit. Besides, she didn't die of her wounds, she drowned. So technically Teresa didn't kill her. They didn't even believe it was attempted murder. Teresa was that convincing. She could definitely be charming when she wanted to be. So, she was off the hook. No arrest or anything.

Adam fired her immediately. No surprise there.

CHAPTER 27

A few days later, Huck and I were hanging out at the cafe after hours, having a snack and gossiping. It was something we did often, with the cafe owner's blessing. She was a sweet woman, in her 70s probably, and I think she thought of Huck as the grandchild she never had. I had met her on several occasions and she even gave me some things for the baby. I never told her I wasn't keeping the baby. I didn't have the heart to try to explain why. She told us she didn't mind if we hung out there and kept an eye on the place. She was so sweet to us.

We were right in the middle of a deep conversation about our future, and trying to come up with a name for the baby, when there was a knock on the door. We both turned to look at the same time and were shocked to see Teresa standing outside watching us. It was locked, so she couldn't just barge in, thankfully. Huck turned to me as if to ask if he should let her in. I just shrugged my shoulders. I was a bit afraid of her, but technically she didn't do anything wrong. She was found to have stabbed Violet in self-defense. I think any of us would have done the same thing if that crazy lady was coming after us with a knife.

Huck walked over and let her in, locking the door behind her.

"Why are you here?" he asked her.

"I want to talk to you," she said, looking over at me a couple of times. "Alone."

"No. Abbey and I are here hanging out. I'm not

going to kick her out because you showed up. What do you want?"

He sounded impatient and I could see that he didn't want Teresa there. She either didn't notice or didn't care.

She looked at me one more time, and motioned with a wave of her hand for Huck to come closer, over to a corner table so they could talk without me hearing. He looked over at me with an apologetic look on his face. I just smiled and went back to my snack. Hopefully she would say what she needed to say and not hang around. I could hear whispering, but not what they were saying.

About three minutes into their conversation, they started getting louder and I turned to look at them, curiously.

"Are you serious?" Huck asked her. "You can't really expect to tell me that you stabbed someone and me not to tell the police. Besides, it was self-defense anyway. So, what's the problem?"

"The problem is that I don't like talking to the cops. Besides, it wasn't really an accident." She looked my way and lowered her voice, but I could still hear her. "The truth is that I went over there to get money out of her about Adam and you know who." Her eyes cast my way and I quickly looked down at my feet. Who was I fooling? "Violet just laughed at me and told me to get out or she would have me arrested for blackmail. That's when I just lost it and stabbed her. That stupid bitch, it was all her fault."

Her voice was getting louder and angrier as I

watched the two of them. I couldn't believe that I just heard her confess to murder. I didn't know what to do. Should I call the cops or just wait until she left to do so? In the end, it didn't matter.

"Let me see if I got this right," I heard Huck say. "It was Violet's fault that you tried to blackmail her and then stabbed her? Oh my god, you are delusional!" he yelled. "I'm calling the cops."

As he turned to walk back toward where I was sitting, I saw her pull a knife out of her pocket and run at Huck. I screamed. Before he could even turn around she plunged the knife into his back. He lurched forward and they both hit the floor. She pulled out the knife as he struggled and stabbed him three more times before I hit her hard in the back of the head with a heavy bowling trophy that had been sitting nearby on the cafe's counter. Teresa was out cold. Huck had been so surprised by her attack that he didn't even have a chance to turn over and defend himself. All of the stab wounds were in his back and he was bleeding profusely.

"Oh my god, Huck, are you okay?" I said as I kneeled down beside him. Stupid question. Of course he wasn't okay.

"Call 911," was all he said before he passed out.

I jumped up and ran for the phone. While I waited for the police to arrive, I unlocked the front door for them. I also kicked the knife away from Teresa, in case she woke up before they arrived. Good thing I did. She woke up a couple of minutes later and tried to get up. I just let her. I didn't need to get into a fight with her, not in my condition. I held tight onto the bowling trophy though, just in case she got the bright idea to come at me. It wasn't necessary though, because she just put her hand to the back of her head, obviously in pain, and walked out the front door without saying a word to me. She didn't even look my way.

As I was watching her leave, I heard Huck start mumbling.

I put my hand on his head to comfort him. "It'll be all right. The ambulance is on the way."

"Abbey." He was a bit slurry. Of course he was, he had lost a lot of blood.

"Yes?" I asked him, while rubbing his head.

"I love you."

"I know, Huck, I know. I love you too." I burst out crying.

"Don't cry. I'll be fine." He was starting to drift off.

"Huck. Stay with me. Huck? Please. Huck wake up!" I yelled.

I checked his pulse, but it was too late. There was nothing I could do. Huck was gone.

That's when the tears started flowing, more than ever. Then I started sobbing. It was the worst moment of my life and I could barely breathe from the gut wrenching sense of loss. I knew at that moment that I blew it. Adam was no good for me. Huck was the one that I really could have loved, if I had given him half a chance. I knew that he loved me. He even said so as he was dying. I had been so stupid. I didn't see what was right in front of me. Huck could have been the love of my life. He would have been a wonderful father to my baby. Now that will never happen. I was the one to blame for that. I should have seen what a mess I was making of my life, pining for a married man that didn't even love me, when I had the most wonderful man right there in front of me.

As I heard the sirens getting louder and louder, getting closer, I suddenly felt a strange sensation in my abdomen. I just dismissed it as stress, or the baby reacting to all the trauma of the night. A couple of minutes later, as the paramedics were running through the front door, I felt it again. I tried to stand up and doubled over in pain. As one of the paramedics checked on Huck, the other came over and asked me if I was all right.

"No, not really. My best friend just died and I'm pregnant. This baby isn't happy about any of it," I wailed.

"Sweetheart, I think you are in labor," he said. "You need to get to the hospital to get checked out. I'll call another ambulance for you."

"I'll take her. It's not an emergency, is it?" a nice looking man, definitely police, but not wearing a uniform, said as he walked into the cafe.

I looked at the man and back to the paramedic. "That's fine, you can go with him. Perez will take care of you," he told me.

"Come on. I'll drive you over to the hospital. I have a few questions to ask you on the way." It didn't seem like I had much choice in the matter.

"Okay." I followed dutifully. I thought that he

looked really familiar. Then I realized that he was the same man that Huck and I passed on the street one day. He was the detective that had his son with him.

As we drove out of the parking lot, he started talking. "What's your name, dear?"

"Abbey," I said quietly.

"How old are you Abbey?"

I thought about lying. I really wanted to say 18, but didn't think he would believe me. Besides, I had no ID to back that up and it would be stupid to lie to the police.

"I'm 16."

"I have a son at home not much older than you. Name's Sam. Where are your parents Abbey?" He was very nice and his questions were friendly sounding, if that's such a thing.

"Um, I'm staying with friends right now." I really didn't want him to call my parents.

He thought for a moment. "I see. Well, we'll get back to that later."

He then proceeded to grill me about Huck and what had happened. It almost sounded like he thought I did it. But, I told him everything about Teresa, Violet, what Teresa confessed to, all of it. I was still having pains all the while, and realized that I was in labor, like the paramedic said. I didn't know if Perez believed me or not, but we arrived at the hospital about that time, so I was through answering questions for a while.

CHAPTER 28

I had the baby that night. All alone. No family. No friends. No one at all to be there with me on what was supposed to be the happiest day of my life.

I didn't call Adam and Sarah until after it was over. I knew it was the last time this baby was going to be all mine. Once I left the hospital I was going to have to share her. She wouldn't even be mine anymore. Since Huck was gone, I knew there was no way I would be able to raise a child on my own. As devastating as it was, I knew in my heart that she was better off with Adam and Sarah. I would do what was right and let my child have a wonderful life. A life that I couldn't give her. A life without me in it.

Before they showed up, I named the baby. I picked out the most wonderful name I could think of and Adam was just going to have to live with it. After I called them, it didn't take long before Adam and Sarah got to my room. They were very fast.

"Why didn't you call us before the baby was born? We wanted to be here," Adam asked as he walked in and over to my bed to take a look at our daughter. He didn't even ask how I was doing.

"There wasn't any time to call. I had her right after I arrived. Besides, I was being interrogated by the police on the ride to the hospital, so I didn't even think about calling. I'm sorry. You should have been here."

Adam and Sarah looked at me with surprise.

"Interrogated about what?" Sarah asked.

"I'll tell you about it later," I told them.

Our happy occasion was not the time for a conversation about my best friend being murdered in front of my eyes. I tried my best not to burst out crying, on the worst and the happiest day of my life. I didn't think such a thing was possible, but it was.

Adam seemed to quickly forget my declaration about being interrogated by the police, as he reached his arms out and I handed the baby to him. "Meet your daughter, Madison," I said as he took her.

I looked at his face for a reaction, hoping he would not fight me on it. Her name was the last thing I would be able to give her and it meant the world to me that she keep it.

He looked up. "You already named her? Madison. I do like it. What do you think, Sarah?" He turned to Sarah and handed my baby to his wife.

"It's a beautiful name," she said, smiling as she took the baby into her arms.

I turned my head as tears began to slide down my cheeks. No one seemed to notice. All eyes were on the new arrival.

"Oh look Adam. She has the same heart shaped birthmark on her neck that you do." They both smiled as I turned back toward them.

Sarah handed the baby back to Adam. "I need to make a phone call. I'll be right back," she told him.

"So," Adam started, "how long are you planning to stay at the ranch now?"

Wow, I had just given birth and he was already

trying to get me out the door.

"Is that your way of asking me to leave?"

"I didn't really mean it to sound that way. But, yeah, I guess. We want to start raising the baby together and things could get really messy with you around. Don't get me wrong, I really appreciate all that you have done. We both appreciate it. I know that it was all unplanned and that I hurt Sarah badly, and that this has got to be the most gut wrenching decision you will ever make, but we are here for you and want to help you out."

He sounded so sincere. Did he really mean everything he was saying or was he just telling me what I wanted to hear? I'm sure he was trying to avoid a fight about leaving my daughter with him and getting out of all of their lives, for good.

"I know that I agreed that you two would raise her, and I plan to stick to that, but I want to stay here. I want to see my daughter grow up, even if I can't be her mother. Please."

I knew it was a long shot, but I had to try. I had serious doubts about it working though.

"I don't think that is a good idea."

Before I had a chance to respond, Sarah walked in with an older gentleman that I didn't know.

"Abbey, this is Dr. Edwin. He's our family doctor," Sarah announced.

The doctor walked over and shook my hand. "Nice to meet you young lady."

"Hi. You too," I responded. I had no idea who he

was and why he was there. "Is something wrong? Why did you bring in a new doctor?"

"No, nothing's wrong," Sarah replied. "Dr. Edwin is going to take care of the birth certificate for us." She looked at me to see my reaction.

"Okay. What do you mean?" I was a bit confused. "This doctor wasn't anywhere around when I gave birth." I hoped it didn't sound rude, because that was not my intention. I just wanted to know exactly what they were doing.

"What I mean is that he is going to put my name on the birth certificate, instead of yours," Sarah replied.

"No one told me you were going to do that." I was getting upset. "Why can't my name be on there?"

If I couldn't keep my baby, I at least wanted my name listed on her birth certificate. I didn't see any problem with that at all. It wasn't like any of their friends were going to see it.

That's when Adam chimed in. "Because Sarah and I will be raising her. It is the same thing as if you were giving her up for adoption to strangers. They always put the adoptive parents' names on the birth certificate."

"Oh, I didn't know that."

So that was that. The doctor put Sarah and Adam as the parents on the birth certificate and signed it. We did live in a small town and they all knew everyone, so it was pretty easy for them to get the people at the hospital to look the other way. Besides, the only people that actually saw me give birth to Madison were the delivery doctor and a couple of nurses. A good chunk of cash and they all forgot everything. It must be nice to have so much money as to get people to do whatever you want.

Because I was doing fine, I was discharged from the hospital a few hours later and rode home with Adam and Sarah. Madison was in the carseat next to me in the backseat, and I couldn't take my eyes off of her. Coming home with my first baby should have been a joyous occasion, but it wasn't. It was all I could do to keep from crying all the way home. I didn't know if Madison would remember anything, it was doubtful of course. But, if there was any chance at all, then I didn't want her only memories of me to be me heartbroken and depressed. I wanted her to remember me happy and loving. I tried my best to show her that. Let me tell you that it is almost impossible to be heartbroken and look happy at the same time.

When we arrived home, they walked into the house to show off their new baby to everyone. No one had a clue that Sarah wasn't her actual mother. She even played it up a bit by walking slowly and sitting gingerly on the couch, like a woman that had just given birth would actually do. I watched her as she did it and rolled my eyes. No one saw me though. No one paid a single bit of attention to me.

I went straight to my room before anyone noticed I was not pregnant. I was in no mood to explain to anyone why I showed up at the ranch no longer pregnant, with no baby in tow.

****

I hid out in my room for a couple of days in a deep

depression. I had lost my best friend, given birth, and given away my own child, all on the same day. Could life get any worse than that? Someone knocked on my bedroom door three times a day and sat a tray of food outside, that I pretty much ignored. I nibbled at it a bit, just so I wouldn't starve, but I had no appetite at all. I only left the room to go to the bathroom and back, and that was it. I didn't see a single soul, and that's the way I wanted it. No one seemed to miss me. I'm sure Adam and Sarah were busy with my baby and were happy that I wasn't around to muddy things up for them.

Finally, I figured I couldn't just stay there forever, so I got up, got a shower and went to the kitchen to see Oliver. I had a plan that needed to be carried out perfectly. He immediately noticed that I was no longer pregnant and his eyes got wide as he looked from my belly up to my face.

"You had your baby?" he asked. "When did that happen?"

"A few days ago." That's all I said. I didn't want to talk about it, but knew that wasn't going to happen.

He put the knife down that he had been using to chop onions, so he could concentrate completely on me.

"What? And you've been in your room all this time? Wait..." He looked at me intently as it finally dawned on him. "Where's your baby?"

Here we go. Luckily I had been rehearsing what I was going to say during all the hours I hid out in my room.

"My parents took him."

"You had a boy?"

"Yes." I was trying to distance my pregnancy from Sarah's baby as much as I could.

"What do you mean that your parents took him? You just let that happen?" His brows furrowed as he was trying to figure out what happened, and why I would do such a thing.

"They didn't take him away from me. That's not what I mean. I gave him to them. For now anyway. I just need some time to figure out what to do with my life and couldn't do that with a baby." It sounded so callous when I said it out loud.

"I see."

No he didn't. He was giving me the strangest look, like I was the worst mother ever, just giving my baby away to my parents like that. Like I didn't even care. If he only knew the truth, he would be completely in shock. Hell, I was completely in shock. The whole thing was so much harder than I ever imagined it would be.

That was enough. I didn't want to talk about it any longer. I knew I would not have to explain my lack of a baby to anyone else. Oliver and his rumor mill would take care of that nicely.

****

A few days later I attended Huck's funeral. I didn't really know if his parents blamed me or not, but they didn't say a word to me. I saw his mother glance over at me once or twice and look away quickly when she saw me watching her. Her behavior toward me was vastly different than when we met at their house.

Because of that, I just sat in the back of the room and stayed out of the way. It was a beautiful service and I could tell that he was deeply loved. So many people were there and got up and said such wonderful things about him. I tried my best not to fall apart.

After the service, I walked home alone, crying the entire way. Whether his parents blamed me or not, I blamed myself. Of course, I didn't kill him, but if I hadn't walked into the coffee house that day, so long ago, fretting over my situation with Violet, this would never have happened. He would never have met Teresa if it weren't for me. I introduced them. How could I not blame myself? It had to be at least a little bit my fault.

That's when I realized that life was delicate. And so short. It saddened me that on the best day of my life, the day I gave birth to my beautiful daughter, that I also lost my best friend. Life would never be the same.

The police arrested Teresa the day after Huck died. She had been hiding out at a friend's house. They had me go to the station and give a detailed account of what I had witnessed. It was enough to charge her with his murder. They told me that she would never be free again. Of course, they still had to have a trial, but it would be a while before that happened. Justice was a very slow process. They couldn't pin Violet's death on her, but at least she would go away for Huck's murder. God, how I missed him.

Over the next few weeks, Sarah and Adam doted on the baby. I was very happy that they adored her, she deserved that in parents. But, it saddened me that I had to pretend to just be an employee there. I was not permitted much contact with her at all. As much as I hated that, I did understand why.

One day I was in the library, pouting and feeling sorry for myself, when Sarah came in. She told me that I couldn't have much contact with the baby because they didn't want anyone to get suspicious. No one knew anything, so it was ridiculous to think that anyone would get suspicious. She asked about my plans and I told her I was working on it. They obviously wanted me out. I just had nowhere to go, so was stalling. I'm sure they could see right through me.

Madison was just adorable. She was chubby with lots of blonde hair. I sneaked in and just watched her in her crib whenever I had the chance. I couldn't be with her anywhere else, so hanging out in her room was my new favorite thing. Usually it was late at night after everyone had gone to bed. One night while I was in there just watching my baby sleep, Adam walked in and freaked out on me.

"What the hell are you doing in here?" he almost yelled.

He was very angry. He walked over, pushed me aside, and looked into the crib like he was expecting her to be gone. Seriously?

"I was just watching her sleep. Nothing else. Nothing is going on in here." I know I sounded defensive. But the way he came thundering in, made me that way.

"Well, you need to leave right now. I don't want you in here anymore."

"I was just looking at her. I don't really see what the big deal is. I love her and just want to be with her from time to time. Can't you understand that?" I really wanted to sound sincere, not argumentative. I didn't want to fight with him.

"Please leave now."

"Okay, fine I'm going."

As I was turning to leave, he stopped me. "I don't want you in here anymore. Do I make myself clear?" He was a little scary.

"Yeah, we'll see about that." And I walked out.

CHAPTER 29

The very next day, I went into town with Oliver to get some cooking supplies. When we arrived home, there was a police car in the driveway. Adam was standing in the driveway talking to the officers and they were writing in their notepads. They all turned to look at us as we pulled up. Oh boy, did he call the cops on me? I didn't know what he could get me for, but he was resourceful. I'm sure he could come up with something. He still had the stolen Picasso hanging over my head. Could that be it? He couldn't possibly think that I would actually take it? Crazy thoughts were racing through my head. He would do anything to get me out.

We did not stop in the driveway, but continued on past them to park around behind the house, where everyone that worked there parked. I tried to put the police out of my mind, figuring that I would hear about it soon enough from someone that worked there. Secrets didn't last long around there.

I was on pins and needles all throughout the dinner preparation and during the meal. Adam didn't say a word to me about the police while I was serving dinner. Not that I expected him to. I was getting a little freaked out by the whole thing. Honestly, the police being there probably had nothing to do with me. If it had something to do with me, I'm sure they would have wanted to question me. But, that didn't happen. I was probably just being paranoid.

After dinner was done and I had finished with all of

the cleanup work, I grabbed some treats for the horses and went for a walk around the ranch to calm my nerves. I ran into Adam in the stables. Not having any desire to fight with him, I just lowered my eyes and walked around him, hoping he would just let me go and not start anything. I was only there to see the horses, not him.

"Abbey, wait," he called after me.

I stopped and turned to face him, saying nothing. What was there to say? We hadn't been getting along very well and I doubted it was going to be any different that time.

"I need to tell you something," he said quietly. It didn't sound like he wanted to start a fight. He was calm.

I waited. I was not going to speak with him if I didn't have to.

"Do you know why the police were here earlier?" he asked me.

"No." I desperately wanted to know, but wasn't about to give him the satisfaction. I could be so stubborn sometimes.

"They were here about the painting. I had to report it stolen."

"I see." I had no desire to engage him in more conversation than that.

"I didn't tell them that I thought it was you."

Was he serious? It sounded like he was trying to let me know that he did me a favor.

"You know it wasn't me. If it was, I would be long

gone from here."

"Maybe." He stood there for a moment contemplating his next move. "Look, I don't really think you took it, and I'm sorry that I accused you. However, my daughter is the most important thing in my life now and I will do anything to keep her here, safe with me."

"What do you mean by that? Why wouldn't she be safe here?" I didn't understand why he thought she would be in any danger.

"You know what I mean. I mean that I want her to stay here with me. Not with you."

"Oh, I see." I stood there for a moment without speaking. "Wait, are you threatening to tell the cops it was me that took the painting, if I take Madison? Is that what this is all about?"

My voice was starting to get higher and higher, because I was starting to freak out some. He was basically telling me that if I took my daughter and left, he would have me put in prison for grand theft. Yes, I was definitely getting freaked out.

"Okay, calm down." He lowered his voice. "The truth is that I don't want to do that. But I need some sort of leverage. I'm afraid that you might take her," Adam told me.

"You do know that she is my daughter, right? I can take her if I want." I had no idea if making threats back at him was going to help the situation or not, but I felt I really had nothing to lose.

"Well, not really. There is no proof that she is your daughter. Sarah's name is on the birth certificate."

That's when he just turned around and walked away, satisfied with himself.

Oh no, he was right. I didn't even think about that. How would I be able to prove that she was really mine? How could I be so stupid as to agree to let them put Sarah's name on the birth certificate, without anything in writing at all to prove she was my biological daughter? Of course, there was DNA, but I would have to convince someone to do a DNA test in the first place. Who would believe me? No one, that's who. Was I the stupidest person ever? I so often jumped into decisions without thinking them through first. It was so reckless, and now I would probably lose my daughter permanently because of it.

A few days later, when no one was around, I went digging in Adam's desk for anything that could help me. Anything at all. I found some paperwork showing that he filed a claim with his insurance company so they could collect the money for the stolen painting. I was pretty sure that it wasn't really stolen, but I had no proof of that. Adam just didn't seem all that upset that a priceless masterpiece was taken from his house. It was something that his grandfather was given as a gift directly from Picasso himself. The sentimental value alone had to be through the roof. Yet, Adam seemed to take it all in stride. What about the fact that someone supposedly broke into their house and knew where to find it? It isn't like it was out in plain sight in the front hallway. It was in a room that most people didn't even know existed. I'm pretty sure Sarah didn't even know that room was in the house. So, why was Adam so calm about the whole thing? If it was my house, and my painting, I would be extremely upset.

Unfortunately my timing was really bad. As I was rifling through Adam's desk, in they walked, both of them. They were talking as they entered the room and didn't even see me at first. I jumped up out of the chair when I heard them approach. The look of guilt on my face had to be priceless.

"What the hell are you doing in here?" Adam was angry, of course. That was his default state where I was concerned.

"Um, nothing. Just looking for a pen." Wow, seriously, that was the best I could come up with?

"What are you holding behind your back?" Sarah asked.

I hadn't even realized I still had the papers in my hand. No point in denying it, I was caught red handed. I brought them around me and held them out for everyone to see.

"Your insurance claim papers, that's what I have. I'm pretty sure that the Picasso was never stolen. I just can't prove it. Not yet anyway," I said smugly, like I had any proof of anything, which I didn't.

"Really? That's all you have, that you are 'pretty sure' it was never stolen? Okay then, let's call the FBI right now." Adam was obviously being very sarcastic.

"Whatever." My clever reply.

"Give me the damn papers." Adam walked over and yanked them out of my hands before I even had a chance to respond.

"Is this what you are going to use to get rid of me? A stolen painting?" I knew the answer before I even asked the question.

"Actually, yes," Sarah jumped in. "We have tried offering you money and you refused it. So, the painting is our next step. Besides we don't know that you didn't take it. You obviously knew about it, knew exactly where it was hung, and now it is gone. You do the math." She glared at me as she made her accusation.

"You know I didn't take it. I wouldn't do that!" I screamed.

"Look at how you are acting. You walk in here and rifle through Adam's desk, then you start screaming at us, like this is our fault," she said mockingly.

"So this is it? You are going to have me arrested for something I didn't do, just to get your hands on my daughter?" I was in shock.

"Our daughter," Sarah said. "She is our daughter, not yours. And we can prove it. You can't prove anything, can you?" She raised her eyebrows and crossed her arms, obviously satisfied with her threat.

"Maybe not right now, but I'll figure out a way."

"Look, Abbey, let me be perfectly blunt with you. You have a record of drug use and theft. Do you actually think anyone would believe someone like you, over someone like me?" Sarah proclaimed.

I suddenly had a fluttery feeling in the pit of my stomach and my breathing became shallow. I'm sure it showed on my face.

"I see that you are surprised that we know about that. Your problem is that you have a big mouth and we have our sources." She was so smug and I wanted to slap her.

Oliver. That's the only person I told. Besides Huck, of course. But Huck wasn't around and he wouldn't have told them anything anyway. I knew it was Oliver. He may not have told Adam or Sarah directly, but was a terrible gossip, so they could have heard my story from just about anyone on the ranch. I should have known better. Stupid, stupid, stupid of me.

"Anyway, we have no qualms about having you arrested for grand theft of the Picasso if you don't leave right away. We mean by tomorrow morning. We will give you some money to live on for a while. We don't want you to starve. But, we will not be supporting you forever. That's up to you. Oh, and just in case we were not clear, you are going alone. Madison stays here," she told me.

"Yeah, I got that," I replied.

CHAPTER 30

I barely slept all that night. I knew my time was up at the ranch. I had to leave in the morning, there really was no choice in the matter. If I didn't leave, I would go to jail, then I would probably never see my baby again, ever. If I left as agreed, then at least there was a chance, albeit a slim one, that I could see her again one day. Maybe when I got older, and Madison was older, they would let me be a part of her life. Probably wishful thinking, but I really couldn't see any other choice in the matter. I knew I had to go. At least for now.

Sometime after midnight I sneaked into the nursery to see her one last time. Well, actually I got to the door of the nursery and was stopped by a huge man wearing a uniform. He was well over six feet tall and considerably more than 200 pounds. I was no match for him. Where the heck did he come from? I couldn't believe that they hired a security guard to watch over the nursery at night. But, when I thought about it, it kind of made sense. Who could blame them for thinking I might sneak in? That's exactly what I was doing. But, I wasn't there to take her, I was there just to see her beautiful face one more time. All that Boris (that's what I decided his name was) had to do was scowl at me and I ran back to my room about as fast as I could. I threw myself on my bed and cried myself to sleep, for about the hundredth time since I had been living on the ranch. I wasn't even going to get the chance to see her again before I left for good.

Very early the next morning the sun was streaming in between the blinds and hit me square in the eyes. Like it or not, I was up. My first thoughts went to my daughter, Madison. How was I ever going to leave her behind? I adored her and couldn't bear to live without her. I knew I was just going to have to deal with it though. Even if I could figure out how to get her out of the house undetected, where would we go? I had no means of support and no one to help us. Besides, I knew they would hunt me down and send me to prison for grand theft, not to mention kidnapping.

So, I packed my things, found Adam and got the money he promised me, and walked out the door. I needed something to survive on and it would last a while. The only person on the ranch I stopped to say good-bye to was Walter. I found him in the stables working. While I was telling him that I was leaving, I burst out crying. Leaving my baby daughter was the hardest thing that I would ever do. I actually thought it might kill me. Walter was very calm and understanding, but there really was nothing he could do. He just hugged me and let me get it all out. He was always so wonderful to me and I was going to miss him.

I was also going to miss Huck. Terribly. By leaving the ranch and the town, I felt like I was leaving him too. He had been such an integral part of my life and it would be a very long time until my broken heart mended, even if just a little.

I figured that Huck's parents didn't care for me, and would be thrilled if they never saw me again, but I wanted to say good-bye to them anyway. Those poor people. They lost both of their children in the worst possible ways. I guess there is no good way to lose your child, but they seemed to get the worst of it. Their daughter, Madison, died at 6 years old from cancer. Then Huck died, sort of because of me. Teresa was the one that stabbed him, but I still felt terrible guilt. When his mother opened the door, she was obviously surprised to see me standing on her front porch.

"Hi. I'm really sorry to bother you, but I just wanted to say that I'm leaving town and how terribly sorry I am about Huck. I didn't get a chance to talk to you at his funeral, so I decided to come by before I left. No matter how you feel about me, I loved him dearly and will miss him for the rest of my life." I just blurted it all out before she had a chance to slam the door in my face. She stood there quietly and let me speak.

"What do you mean 'no matter how you feel about me'?" she asked.

"Just that I'm kind of responsible for him getting killed, and you probably hate me for it. That's all." I looked at my feet in a desperate attempt not to cry.

"Oh, sweetheart. You are not responsible at all. We don't blame you. Why would you think that?" She sounded so kind.

I looked up at her then. I could see the sincerity on her face.

"You don't? I thought you hated me, because I was the one that introduced him to Teresa."

"No, of course not. How could you have known?

Besides, we know how much Huck loved you. He talked about you all the time." She smiled at me then.

"He did?"

"Yes. He was in love with you. You know that, right?"

"Yeah, I know. I so wish things had been different," I told her.

We both took a moment to reflect on that.

"So, I heard you had your baby. But that's all I know. Boy or girl?" She was trying to change the subject, which I was thankful for.

I smiled when thinking of my beautiful daughter. "A girl. I named her Madison." I desperately hoped that his mother would be okay with that.

"You did?" She was definitely surprised.

"Yes. Huck talked so often, and with so much love, about his little sister. Then he died on the day my daughter was born. I wanted to honor him somehow. I hope you don't mind." I held my breath, waiting for her reaction.

"Oh wow. Absolutely not. I don't mind at all. I'm so honored that you did that. Huck would be thrilled."

She leaned over and gave me a strong, reassuring hug. I hugged her back tightly. When she let me go, she had a sad, kind of soulful look on her face. I knew her children were both on her mind.

"I wanted to let you know that we have decided to move out of state," she told me. "We need a fresh start and we are leaving tomorrow. It is just too hard for us to stay here, especially in this house. Too many memories, you know?"

I knew.

"I understand. That's why I'm leaving too. It's so hard being here and not having Huck around. I need a fresh start too," I told her.

I left then, promising to keep in touch, knowing that would probably not happen. People promise, and probably mean it at the time, but keeping in contact long distance was something that most people just weren't very good at. Especially me. I knew it was most likely the last time I would see her. I would remember her forever though. She was the mother of the best guy I had ever known and I named my daughter after her own daughter. That made her family special to me.

****

I'm ashamed to admit it, but it didn't take me long to find my old friends and get back into my old drug habits. They were all still in the same place, the ones that were still alive anyway, so they weren't hard to find. At first, I just wanted to be with people that knew me, and actually liked me. It was such a welcome change from the horrible people I had been living with for the last year. I got pretty good at hiding out too. I didn't want my parents to find out I was nearby, so I stayed indoors mostly, hanging out with people they didn't know.

I really didn't intend on using drugs, had actually told myself that I wouldn't. But I did. I fell right back into the same old thing. It was such an idiotic thing to do. I know that now. I knew it then. I just didn't care enough to do anything about it. My life had completely fallen apart. It was such a reckless life that I was leading and I felt there was no way out.

Whenever I was sober, and had time to think about my daughter, I just lost it. She was growing up without me and it was all my fault. I allowed it to happen. All of it. I know I was young, but that's no excuse for stupidity. I didn't have to be a victim. However, I let it happen anyway. I let Violet manipulate me. I let Adam seduce me. I let Sarah take my baby and pass her off as her own. I let all of it happen and I was the only one to blame. The only time my mind was at rest from all of those horrible thoughts was when I was high. It was my only solace from reality.

I had friends, I guess. They sort of came and went over time. Some got out of the lifestyle and some died. Most of them would live like that for the rest of their lives, because no one seemed to care about helping them make a change. I seemed to be one of the people that would never get out. I knew the repercussions of what I was doing and just didn't care. Without Madison, life was not worth living. I would never kill myself deliberately, but I knew that what I was doing would probably result in my death anyway. I wanted out so badly, but didn't really have the drive to do it myself. So, that's how I lived, or just existed actually, for the next two years.

****

Early one morning I woke up, hungover, on a mattress that had been thrown on the floor for me in a crappy apartment that wasn't even mine. There were several people passed out around me. So pathetic. I just laid there for several minutes, taking in the scene. What was I doing? I couldn't live like that anymore. I would die if I kept it up, that was a fact. As I lay there, my thoughts drifted to my daughter, as they inevitably did, and as I realized what day it was, overwhelming sadness washed over me. That's the moment that I decided 'today is the day'. It was the day that I was going to get my life back on track. It was Madison's second birthday and I decided at that moment that I was going to be a better person. I had not seen or heard anything about her in all that time, and now I wanted things to be different.

It took some time, but I found a rehab facility that would take me for free. It was a government sponsored program to help get people off the streets and get them started on a better life. I vowed that it would be the last time I ever did any type of drug, and the last time a rehab facility would see my face. Those were the most horrible weeks of my life, but I got through them. I survived somehow. Once my head and body were clear of everything, I needed a life plan. What was I going to do? Where would I get a job, a place to live, a life? Would Madison be a part of any of that?

Once I was clearheaded and out of rehab, the facility helped me get a job. It wasn't much, just a cashier at a restaurant, but it was a start. I worked hard and thought that maybe one day I could be the chef there. A pipe dream, probably. I worked for a few weeks to save up some money, before I decided to move forward with my plan.

CHAPTER 31

I decided that I wanted my daughter back with me. It was time and I was tired of messing around and letting people manipulate me. Things needed to change. I didn't know exactly how I was going to accomplish my goal of getting Madison back, but I had to try. I borrowed a friend's car and drove to the ranch with just one goal in mind. How I hoped I wouldn't end up in jail after all was said and done.

I drove right up to the front door of the ranch and walked into the house without knocking. What was the point in announcing myself first by knocking on the door? They would have never let me in. I figured the best place to find Adam was in the library and that's exactly where he was. Funny how things never change. He looked up from his desk as I walked in. It took just a couple of seconds for recognition to register on his face. He scowled immediately. I didn't care. Then his eyes darted to something on the floor. I followed his gaze. That's when I saw her. My daughter, Madison. She was sitting on the floor coloring in a book, with the nanny sitting nearby. She looked up and smiled at me. She was the most beautiful person I had ever seen. Emotion just washed over me, and I quickly realized that tears were streaming down my face.

"Please take her to the nursery," Adam instructed the nanny, as he got up and walked around his desk in an obvious attempt to stop me from doing anything.

There was no need for me to argue. I knew that would be futile. I just stood there watching her as she was carried out, waving to me as she went. I smiled and waved back. He stood and watched me intently until they left. He probably thought I was going to grab her and run. I would never do that. She didn't know me and scaring her was the last thing I wanted to do that day.

Once they were out the door, he started in on me. "Abbey, why are you here? I never expected to see your face again," he told me bluntly as he went back and sat down behind his desk.

I snapped out of it and turned to face him, wiping my face with the sleeve of my shirt.

"Nice to see you too. How have you been Adam?" a little sarcastic, perhaps, but I was hoping to break the ice before the real conversation began.

"Abbey. What do you want?" I guess he wasn't going to play along.

"I want to talk to you about Madison. I want her back. Or at least joint custody."

I wasn't stupid enough to think that Adam would just hand her over, no questions asked. Joint custody was fair. Even after everything, I wanted to be fair. Besides, no judge would take her from the only parents she's ever known and give her to a stranger, biological mother or not.

"You have got to be kidding me."

"Adam, she's my daughter. I'm older now. I have a job and can take care of her. Please, can't we just talk about it?" I pleaded. "I just want to try and work this out, like adults."

"Absolutely not." He didn't even hesitate. It sounded like a final answer to me, and I'm sure that's the way he meant it.

"Adam, please, be reasonable. She has a right to know her mother, doesn't she?" I tried my best not to sound like I was begging, but it probably sounded that way anyway.

"She knows her mother. Sarah is her mother." He certainly wasn't backing down. Not that I expected him to.

"I know. I'm sure Sarah is good to her, but shouldn't she know the truth? Do you want her to find out later by accident? At some point she will find out."

"Abbey," he said seriously as he walked around from behind his desk again and stood right in front of me, "let me be perfectly clear. You need to leave right now, and if I ever see you again, I will kill you myself." He said it slowly and methodically.

I believed that he would carry out his threat if I didn't do as he said. I may have once loved him, but not this person. Not this version of him. He terrified me. I didn't say a word to him. I just turned around and walked out. I would have to figure something else out. I'm sure Adam was convinced that that was the last he was going to see of me. It wasn't. I just wasn't sure exactly what my next move would be.

Then the strangest thing happened. As I was walking past one of the many rooms in the house, toward the front door, someone reached out and tugged my shirt. It made me jump. I turned to see Sarah holding up her index finger to her lips, shushing me.

Against my better judgment I followed her into the room. She closed the door behind us and we walked to the far end of the room to talk.

Still keeping her voice low, she said to me, "I saw you come in. Why are you here?"

"I came to talk to Adam about joint custody of Madison. Why are we whispering?"

"Obviously I don't want anyone to hear. I have a proposition for you," she replied.

This ought to be good.

"I will give you a lot of money if you come back later and kidnap Madison."

Then she stood there waiting for my reaction.

"What? Are you serious? Why would you do that?" I was thoroughly confused by her offer.

"I know this sounds harsh, but the truth is that I don't want to raise someone else's child. It just isn't the same as having my own. Besides, Adam dotes on her and pretty much ignores me. I hate her for that. I hate Madison and all that she represents: his affair with you and the fact that he was in love with you, and how he was able to have a child with you and not me. I know it's harsh, but I just can't help the way I feel. If I can get rid of her, things will change around here."

I couldn't believe what I was hearing. I thought that she finally lost her mind. I stood there trying to process what she had said, what she had offered.

"Abbey? Did you hear me?" She waved her hand in front of my face to get my attention.

That snapped me out of it. "Oh, sorry. Yes, I heard

you. This is a joke, right?" She had to be joking. There was no way it was legitimate. "Does Adam know what you're planning?"

"Of course not. Don't be an idiot." She rolled her eyes at me.

Yeah, that was a stupid question.

"Did your mother drop you on your head as a child?" I don't think she was trying to be funny.

I just glared at her. "Can I go to prison for kidnapping my own daughter? I mean, people don't even know she is my daughter." It was a fair question.

I have to admit that the idea of getting Madison back thrilled me. She would be all mine. They still didn't know my real last name. It would be difficult for Adam to find me. But I was terrified at the same time. I knew that he would never just let her go without a fight. He would call the police the second he discovered her missing. I would have to spend my life on the run. Was that fair to Madison? She didn't deserve that type of life. No, I couldn't do that to her, could I? If Sarah did give me a lot of money, like she said, I could afford to hide out in style. Madison would probably never know that people were looking for us. I really wished that I had some time to seriously think all of it through. There were a lot of consequences to what Sarah was planning. I didn't go to the ranch planning to kidnap my daughter. I was there to try to work out some type of custody arrangement with Adam. But, as I stood there I realized he would never agree to that. Taking her might be my only option. It scared the daylights out of me though.

"I don't know. This sounds like a really bad idea to me." I was waffling.

"Do you want your daughter back or not?" Sarah was clearly getting impatient with me.

It was a serious question. I could tell by the tone in her voice that she meant it. She wanted nothing more than to get rid of Madison.

"Yes, of course. But…"

She cut me off. "Just stop. Don't be so afraid of every little thing. I'm going to help you. I promise that this will work."

CHAPTER 32

They never locked the doors at the ranch, which was shocking to me, especially with a toddler in the house. I guess they figured there was no reason to bother on an estate that big with employees milling around all the time. No one would ever get in without being seen.

Per Sarah's instructions, at 2 a.m. sharp I drove around to the back of the estate with my headlights off. I parked on the other side of a large van that belonged to one of the staff that lived there. No one would be able to see my car that way, if anyone was up at that hour and happened to look out one of the windows. I got out of my car quietly and skulked to the back door. I crept down the hallway quietly without anyone seeing me. I think I held my breath the whole way. It was very dark and a bit scary creeping through the house in the middle of the night, knowing I could get caught at any moment. Before I got to Madison's room, I heard someone moving around. I stopped and pressed my back up to one of the closed hallway closet doors and tried to make myself very small and invisible, in case they walked past me in the dark hallway. No one did though. I heard them go into the hall bathroom and I stood there for several minutes waiting for them to finish up and get back to their bedroom. It had to be one of the staff that lived there. Adam and Sarah had a bathroom in their room, so would have no reason to go out into the hallway. Finally it was quiet again and I continued on my way.

When I reached the nursery, it too was very quiet. Apparently Boris didn't work there anymore. No need, I guess, since I had left long ago. Sarah had packed a few of Madison's things and I found the suitcase in the closet where she left it. I had to feel around for it, because I didn't want to turn on any lights. Luckily there was a dim nightlight in the room so I could see Madison lying in her bed peacefully. She must have seen me too, because just as I walked toward her she started crying. I panicked.

"Oh sweetheart, please be quiet. We don't want to wake anyone up," I said to her softly, trying to calm her down. It didn't work. Of course it didn't work. I was a complete stranger to her, sneaking into her room in the middle of the night. That would freak anyone out. Poor baby.

I picked her up gently, hoping to quiet her. Just as I did, Adam walked in and flipped on the light. My eyes immediately slammed shut on their own, against the shocking lights hitting them all of a sudden.

"What the hell?" Adam was definitely surprised to find me standing there, holding our daughter. "Give her to me." He walked across the room quickly and yanked her out of my arms. That just made Madison scream even louder. "Now look what you've done!" he yelled at me.

"What I've done? I was calming her down and you came storming in here, flipped on the lights and grabbed her from me. That's why she is crying."

"Why are you here?" he asked as he laid her back down in the crib and covered her up. That's when he looked down and saw the suitcase sitting on the floor next to me. "What is going on?"

"I told you earlier, I'm here for my daughter. You are completely unreasonable and since you won't even talk to me about some sort of joint custody, I'm taking her." I tried to sound forceful, hoping he would take me seriously.

Just then, Sarah walked in and feigned shock at seeing me there. She was pretty convincing. I almost believed that she was surprised to see me.

"You are trespassing and I'm calling the police. Sarah stay here with her until I get back. And don't let her near my daughter," he told her as he turned to leave.

Sarah just shook her head in disbelief when he said 'my daughter,' and not 'our daughter.' She then walked over and stood by the crib, keeping up with her performance. She had to make sure he had no clue that she was involved in my taking Madison.

"Yeah, you do that. I'm sure they would be happy to know that you were sleeping with your 15 year old employee. And here's the proof," I said smugly, pointing at Madison.

That stopped him in his tracks. He turned around to face me.

"You wouldn't dare." He looked a little scared.

"Wouldn't I?"

He stood there for a moment, probably trying to decide if I was bluffing or not. I wasn't.

"You know that I can still tell the cops that you

stole the Picasso."

"Go ahead. You already told the police that you didn't know who took it. There's no proof that I did. They won't believe you when I tell them that you were blackmailing me with that painting, so I would leave my daughter with you."

The look on his face was priceless. I think he finally realized that he had nothing to hold over me. I held all the cards, thanks to Sarah and her coaching. She told me exactly what to say to make this happen, in case I got caught. I could tell it was starting to work. Sarah just stood there. When I looked over at her, she had a slight, almost imperceptible smile on her face.

"I'm not letting you leave this house with my daughter." He started to come closer, trying to intimidate me. He reached out and grabbed my arm, which I quickly yanked away from him.

That's when I lost my mind. I had a knife in my pocket that I brought just in case things went sour. I grabbed it out of my pocket and shoved Adam up against the wall, completely taking him off guard. Then I held it up to his throat before he had a chance to react. I had to be strong. I knew that if I waffled at all, he would overpower me easily.

"Let me make something clear," I told him. "I'm taking my daughter tonight, and if you ever touch me or her again, I will kill you. I have nothing to lose if I don't have my daughter, so going to prison for your murder does not scare me. And, if you come after us, I will absolutely tell the cops everything about how I got pregnant at 15 years old, against my will, by my boss.

Then you will be spending a lot of time in prison. Got it?" I said every word slowly, for emphasis.

"Yeah, I got it." He looked like he was really afraid of me at that moment. I'm pretty sure he believed every word I said.

Sarah never said a word as I backed away from Adam and put the knife back in my pocket. Then I picked up Madison and the suitcase and walked out the door, keeping my eyes on him the entire time. Adam didn't move or say another word to me. As I was heading down the hallway, I heard Adam and Sarah bickering. He sounded very angry that she just stood there and did nothing to help him or stop me from taking Madison.

I was absolutely sure that he would come after me at some point. I was smart enough to know that. He couldn't just let his daughter disappear in the middle of the night and not tell anyone. People would notice. Luckily he had no idea that Sarah was in on the whole thing. She gave me a nice chunk of money to disappear for a while. It wouldn't last forever, but was a very nice start.

Even with the money Sarah gave me, I really had nowhere to go. Other than my family and drug addict friends, I didn't know anyone outside of the ranch. And I was not about to go back to that way of life with my daughter in tow. That was a vow I made to myself when I went into rehab for the very last time. No matter how hard things got, drugs were part of my past for good. So, I decided to go home.

When we arrived at my parents' house, very early

in the morning, the sun was just peaking up over the mountains and it was still mostly dark outside. I knocked on the front door. I didn't feel like I should just walk in, because I didn't live there anymore. Besides, I didn't want to frighten my parents by barging in the front door so early in the day. They might still be in bed. They were early birds though, so I doubted they would be asleep.

When the door opened, my mother's face went from just a touch of confusion to a huge smile, then the tears came as she grabbed me and hugged me like it had been years since she saw me last. Three years, to be exact. She was so emotional that she didn't even notice Madison standing next to me, holding my hand.

After holding on to me for a full minute, she let me go and backed up a bit while wiping the tears from her face.

"Abbey, come in." She moved aside to allow me to enter the house. That's when she saw Madison. "Oh my goodness, who is this?" She looked down at Madison and back up to me, just as realization took hold. "You have a daughter?" She smiled.

"Yes." That was the first thing that I said since my mother opened the door. I was trying very hard to keep it all together. "This is Madison. Sweetheart, this is your grandma." I picked up Madison so she could get a better look.

"She's beautiful, Abbey. Oh, I almost forgot your father. Leland!" she yelled to the kitchen. "Come in here quick."

My father almost ran in. "What's the matter? Are

you all ri...?" The words just hung there as he realized it was me standing there. "Abbey!"

He started crying immediately. I handed Madison to my mother and ran to my father's arms. I didn't even realize until that moment how much I missed my family. We were all crying by then and even Madison started crying. That made me laugh.

"Oh honey, it's okay. I'm fine," I said, taking her from my mother. "Dad, I want you to meet your granddaughter, Madison."

"Hi Madison, sweetheart. I'm happy to know you," he said in a gentle voice. He took her hand and kissed it. That made her smile. "I think she likes me," he said to me. "She and I are going to get along famously."

I loved the fact that neither of my parents seemed upset that I came back with a two year old. They never said a word about me getting pregnant at such a young age. I think they were just happy that I came back and was all right.

It didn't take us long to get settled in. Madison and I moved into my old bedroom and were very comfortable there. I found a job in a local restaurant and my parents watched Madison while I was at work. They didn't mind at all. They adored and spoiled her. Madison took to them right away.

Everything seemed to be going very well, until a few days after our arrival when I went outside and picked up the newspaper for my father. He read it every morning with his coffee. He had been doing that as long as I could remember. Then I saw the lead story. There was a huge photo of Madison on the front page.

The article said that they believed the housekeeper (I was not the housekeeper) kidnapped their daughter out of her bed, while everyone was sleeping. There was no mention of Adam and Sarah catching me in the nursery on the night I took her. It said there was a massive search, with hundreds of volunteers, who turned up no leads. They offered a reward of $100,000 for any tips leading to her whereabouts. The name of the housekeeper in the story was Abigail Hunter and I was the prime suspect because I had recently been fired. They believed it was a fake name, which it was. It said Madison was the only child of Adam and Sarah Tyler. They had no credible leads.

The story also mentioned the heart shaped birthmark on her neck, by her left ear. It was a perfect match for Adam's birthmark.

There was no way I could let my parents see the article. They might put two and two together. Well of course they would. There was a photo of Madison right there with the story, and the birthmark was a dead giveaway. I removed the front page of the paper and threw it away. When I handed it to my dad, I told him that it got wet. He could still read the rest of the paper and I would get him a new one when I went into town later. Of course, I never did and he forgot all about it as he went on about his day.

The crises was averted, temporarily anyway.

CHAPTER 33

Unfortunately, over the next few weeks the media coverage didn't go away. It definitely slowed way down, as things like that do, but it still showed up in the newspaper occasionally. I made a point of getting up very early every single morning to check the paper before my father got a hold of it. Later articles just mentioned the kidnapping, but they were on later pages and easy to hide from my dad. All of the deception was starting to wear thin.

One morning my parents left to go do some shopping, as they did every single Sunday morning of my life. Funny how things never change. Madison was in her high chair working on some oatmeal I had made for her, and making a horrible mess. You can just imagine a two year old and oatmeal. The doorbell rang and I went to answer it, leaving Madison in the kitchen while I went to the front door. When I opened it, I was shocked. There stood Sarah. She just smiled at me.

"What are you doing here?" I wasn't very friendly. I'm sure she had no expectation that I would be.

"What kind of way is that to greet the person that gave you a small fortune and everything that you want?" she snidely remarked as she walked past me into the house. Her eyes scanned the room, obviously looking for something.

I followed her as she walked toward the kitchen, apparently oblivious to anyone that might be in the house and see her. She walked into the kitchen and smiled when she saw Madison.

"Hi sweetheart," Sarah said to her in her best impression of a mother.

"Mommy!" Madison reached for her and Sarah turned her back on her to talk to me.

Poor Madison. She had no idea what that was all about. To her, Sarah was her mother, the only one she had ever known. Until I showed up. She had been with me for a few weeks by that time, and I'm sure she loved me too. However, she had lived her whole life with Sarah. She didn't understand that Sarah was not really her mother. I knew over time that would change. She was young enough to forget all about Sarah and come to love me as her only mother. It might take a little while for that to happen though.

"Sarah, how did you find me?"

I had no idea how she could have possibly found me. I had used a fake name. I know that I never told anyone, except Huck, where I was from, and he swore to keep my secret to the end. Strange that that's exactly what happened. At least there was this one thing I kept my big mouth shut about.

"Teresa told me."

"What? She did? Since when do you talk to her? Isn't she in prison?" That whole family hated Teresa for stabbing Violet. It seemed unlikely anyone had any contact with her after all she had done.

"Stop asking me a million questions." She put her hand up toward me, for emphasis. "I went to visit her in prison. We had a chat. I would never have found you if you had kept your big mouth shut and not told her everything. Luckily for me you did tell her," she smirked.

Oh yeah, I had completely forgotten that I told those things to Teresa in confidence. I guess Huck wasn't the only one I told. Teresa and I had been friends once. I guess I did have a big mouth.

"Why would she tell you anything?" Teresa hated that family as much as I did. It seemed unlikely that she would even talk to Sarah.

"Because I accused her of stealing the painting. With that and the stabbing of Violet, it could go very badly for her. I don't know if you are aware, but she only got 15 years for killing your friend, Huck. Crime of Passion and all that. Add grand theft to the mix and she might never get out. I reminded her of that." Sarah seemed very satisfied with herself.

"Wow, you are getting a lot of mileage out of that stupid missing painting."

"Yes I am. In fact, I could still use it against you if I wanted to. You left our house and somehow came into a lot of money for someone with no job. I wonder how that would look to the police?"

"Did you just come here to threaten me, or is there some purpose to your visit?" I said through clenched teeth.

"I came to pick up my daughter." She turned and looked at Madison, scrunching her face up at my daughter all covered in oatmeal, then looked back at me. "You'll need to clean her up first though. I can't put her in my car like that."

"What! Hell no." I jumped in between her and Madison. "I thought you couldn't wait to get rid of her."

"True. But now there is so much publicity about her kidnapping, it is starting to worry me. I'm afraid someone will find out I'm responsible. Besides, Adam talks of nothing but her. I thought that getting rid of her would make our marriage better, but it has gotten worse. Adam is never going to stop looking for her. I figured that if I came and got her, maybe we could figure out how to be a happy family."

"No. Not gonna happen. Besides, how in the world are you going to explain where she came from? If you tell them I took her, then I will make sure everyone knows you paid me a lot of money to do so. They will also learn that I am her mother, not you." I was desperate.

"No one will believe you. My doctor will vouch for me."

She was still holding on to the fact that her name was on Madison's birth certificate, not mine. I didn't care about that anymore. I would prove Madison was mine, no matter what it took.

"You've heard of DNA, right?" I asked her. She was a doctor after all.

"Shut up." She shoved me aside and reached for Madison.

Without even thinking, I grabbed a handful of her hair and yanked her backward as hard as I could, causing her to stumble several feet across the floor and land face down. I jumped in between her and Madison while Sarah was recovering.

She quickly got to her feet. "Get out of my way.

I'm taking her."

"The hell you are." I grabbed a pair of scissors that were laying on the kitchen counter and held them in front of me.

Sarah stopped dead in her tracks. "What? Are you going to stab me now?" She gave me a one sided grin. She obviously was not afraid of me as she came closer.

"You better believe it. Come one step closer. I dare you." I tried my best to say it with confidence. I wasn't sure it worked.

She did stop though. She looked at the scissors, then back at me, then at Madison.

"I don't believe you have the nerve. You wouldn't stab me in front of my daughter." She stepped toward me.

That's when I knew that I better act fast. It was her or me. That was clear. I lunged at her and cut her arm as she twisted away from me.

"You bitch!" she screamed as she looked at her bleeding arm.

"I told you I was serious. Stay away from my daughter. She's mine, not yours." I wasn't about to go down without a fight.

"You are not going to actually stab me with those things. You want to go to prison, and never see Madison again?"

"Yes, if that's what it takes. Besides, if I let you take her, I won't see her again anyway. So what do I have to lose?"

She hesitated another moment. She was definitely

contemplating whether I had the nerve to actually stab her or not. I guess she decided to chance it because she lunged at me again. That's when I stabbed her in the shoulder. I did that on purpose. I didn't want to kill her. I just wanted to scare her into leaving. She dropped to the floor in pain, holding her shoulder and being very dramatic about the whole thing.

"Get me a towel, before I bleed to death!" she screamed at me.

I obeyed, hanging onto the scissors the whole time. I didn't trust her for a second.

"Are you going to leave my house now, or not?" I held up the scissors in front of me, for emphasis.

She hesitated for just a moment, obviously contemplating the likelihood that I would actually do some real damage next time.

"Fine, I'm going. You know, you could really hurt someone with those things."

"That's the idea," I replied. "Don't ever come back. I will kill you next time." She knew I meant it.

After she left, I quickly started cleaning up the mess before my parents arrived home to see the carnage. Even though the slice on her arm and the stab to the shoulder weren't that bad, she was a bleeder, and it took a while to get it all cleaned up. It was amazing to me that Madison just sat there and watched the whole thing without saying a word. I was surprised that she wasn't crying after seeing me attack the only mother she knew. But she was very calm about it all.

I knew that Madison was having a great time at our new house and my parents just adored her. I, unfortunately, was terrified the entire time we were living there. I just knew that the police were going to show up at any moment and drag me away, never to see my daughter again, especially after my encounter with Sarah. I couldn't let that happen. Madison did not deserve that, nor did my parents. So, I took matters into my own hands and left on my own. It was the hardest thing I have ever done, because I knew I would probably never see her, or them, again. The safest place I could think to leave Madison was with my parents. I couldn't take her with me and have her live her life on the run. That was not fair to her and no way for a little girl to live. She deserved a nice, quiet life, out of harms way.

I was positive that Sarah would never return and my parents would raise her right. I know I didn't turn out all that great, for a few years anyway, but that was my fault, not theirs. They were good people and she would be happy and safe with them.

That night I quietly packed the few things I had, kissed my baby on the forehead for the very last time, and walked out the door.

Even though it was the hardest thing I would ever do in my entire life, in my heart I knew it was the right decision. She was safe and that's all that mattered.

A NOTE FROM THE AUTHOR

I hope you enjoyed reading A Reckless Life as much as I enjoyed writing it.

An author's success depends on readers like you. The best way to reach more readers is to have a whole bunch of feedback. So, if you liked my book, please take just a moment to leave me a review.

You can find the review page by going to my website below and clicking on the book.

If you enjoyed this book and would like information on new releases, sign up for my newsletter here:

MichelleFiles.com

Thank you!
Michelle

CPSIA information can be obtained
at www.ICGtesting.com
Printed in the USA
LVHW080930150521
687527LV00015B/952